HOWARD

BE THY

NAME

A Novel

JOANN STEVELOS

For my family and friends,

You are my home now.
In your love, my salvation lies.

"Under an Orange Sky"
by Alexi Murdoch

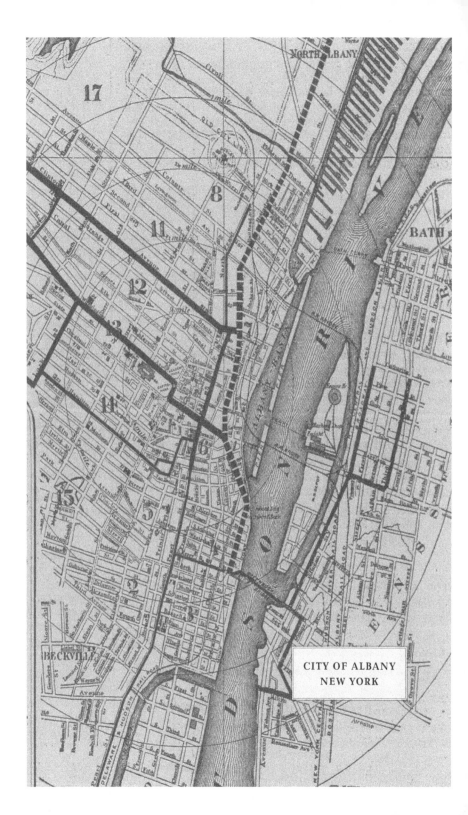

CITY OF ALBANY
NEW YORK

TABLE OF CONTENTS

CHAPTER ONE

2017

Thep were there at the red light for what seemed a long time. A time longer than any other time JoBeth could remember: longer than waiting for a kettle to whistle, or than getting her teeth cleaned, or waiting for flights in security lines. Longer than childbirth, or watching her grandmother die.

CHAPTER TWO

1972

JoBeth sat in the back seat of the rose-colored Cadillac. A small cloth pocketbook packed with a tooth brush, a comb, a purple headband, extra socks, and a dog-eared copy of Harriet the Spy was wedged between her knees. Her older sister, Susan, was in front with Evie, their mother. None of them spoke. Evie gripped the white leather steering wheel, and chewed on the tip of a Virginia Slim as the smoke billowed around her lips.

They waited at a red light.

JoBeth focused on a long line of customers at the corner ice cream shack that moved slowly. She watched a father as he lifted a boy smaller than JoBeth to the counter; both the father's arms were wrapped tightly around the black-haired boy. Small woven sandals dangled from the boy's feet, swinging impatiently against his father's thigh. The father handed the boy a strawberry swirl with sprinkles. JoBeth always preferred vanilla.

JoBeth cracked the window to catch her breath as the smoke from Evie's lungs lifted around her and seeped out the tiny opening. *Tie a Yellow Ribbon Round the Ole Oak Tree* played loudly in the car behind them. Susan stared straight ahead from her post in the front seat, pulled her knee socks up, a nervous habit, and pulled her pink floral shirt away from her sweaty belly. Evie glanced at JoBeth in the rearview mirror, her lips now slack around the cigarette. The glance was more of a slap than a look of concern, and JoBeth felt it sting as such. JoBeth had seen that look of Evie's many times, more so than the other children. Her eyes taunted you, dared you to say what was true rather than stay silent, complicit in her lie or tangled narrative.

JoBeth felt her shorts creep up her backside and wiggled to adjust them. She wished she had remembered to pack her blue denim bell bottoms, they fit her better, and she liked how the bells swished across the ground when she jumped rope.

Outside of the window, JoBeth watched the nice seeming father as he paid for the ice cream his son devoured. She tucked Howard's white crystal rosary into her summer jacket's front pocket. Earlier JoBeth had packed her suitcase with her clothes, carried it to the garage, and loaded it into the trunk. JoBeth reached down and slipped her right shoe back on. It had fallen from her foot in the rush to climb into the car; just after she had stood by the door dumbfounded as she witnessed her mother and sister ransack their home of jewelry, furs, silver, and cash from Howard's secret room in the basement.

Evie's shameless indifference to the gravity of the situation crushed what was left of JoBeth's dignity when she turned and screamed at JoBeth, "Tell me he didn't!" then whispered, "Did he?"

The words, from Evie's hungover mouth, were fierce with condemnation, and hung in the air like a noose. The light was still red as JoBeth nodded yes. Yes — JoBeth thought as she closed her eyes, knowing that Evie already knew the answer, and had known the answer to her question for a very long time. Evie had known the answer when *between evening and morning* she heard Howard's footsteps leaving JoBeth's room. She had known the answer was yes when she placed a Band-Aid on JoBeth's bruised neck after too much 'horseplay' with Howard. Evie knew, and had forsaken her — and now she demanded JoBeth pretend she didn't know — which hurt JoBeth more than anything Howard had ever done to her.

The boy licked his strawberry swirl. The sweltering July heat bore in through the open window. The song from the car behind them ended. The crystal rosary beads were sharp against JoBeth's chest. After her first communion, Howard had given her the rosary and a bouquet of white roses, the tightly wrapped buds were frosty white and delicate as virgin snow.

Evie turned to face JoBeth, her neck bright with the sun, a bead of sweat dropped from her forehead onto the white leather headrest. Evie's eyes widened with defiance; her jowls quivered with rage. Evie demanded a different answer than the one JoBeth had given as JoBeth folded forward, rested her face on her knees, and shut her eyes. Heartsick, JoBeth wished to disappear — to just die.

After the light turned green, they headed to Evie's cousin's house. Rosemary was a hairdresser and married to a plumber, Nino. Evie thought it a garish house; a brown double-wide trailer with plastic yellow shutters.

Evie told Susan and JoBeth to wait in the car, "I will be right back. Don't you dare breathe a word of this to Rosemary. Let me do the talking." Susan nodded for both of them and waited for Evie to get to the door before she climbed over the seat and sat with JoBeth. Susan inhaled a long breath and slowly released it. She had stopped breathing at the red light. She could no longer pretend that she, or the other children, would ever escape the chaos Evie had created to live with Howard. Unlike Evie, Susan understood the gravity of what had happened between Howard and JoBeth and wished that Vinnie was with them to help her ward off any potential consequences.

Susan had secretly hated Evie for a long time and now she had even more reason to despise her. Susan simply preferred her father's company and that had always caused tension between mother and daughter. At the red light, Susan lost any hope that Evie might do the right thing one day; that their situation would improve if she just gave it time, as Evie had begged her to do so often. Evie had severed ties with all that Susan loved; her school, her home in Albany, her grandparents, and then finally her father when she moved them to a suburb to live in secret with Howard. As much as Evie wanted all of them to pretend that Howard was their father, and not a priest, her desire, in the face of reality made it less and less sustainable despite her intent to continue to live the life of luxury they all had grown accustomed to.

Susan remembered the day she learned Howard had assumed their estranged father's identity. Howard and Evie sat them all down in the new house and told them that from now, in their new home, they would call Howard—Dad. But, that they had to remember to call him Father Howard while they were at church. Evie told JoBeth and Michael, being younger and less likely to have good recall, to call him Charlie Brown if they couldn't remember. However, in their new neighborhood, he introduced himself using their father's last name, which was Korli. Howard became Mr. Korli, just like their Dad. He told all their neighborhood friends to just call him Howard, "There is no need for formalities in this house," he would say as he shook their hand or patted them on the back.

Susan, not JoBeth or Michael, was the one who first called Howard — Charlie Brown. During dinner one night, Susan had told Evie and Howard about a homework assignment. The class had been asked to share what their father did for a living.

"Who wants to know, sweetie?" Evie asked, her voice strained to be light and interested. Howard rested his fork and knife on his plate and stared at Evie as he waited for Susan to reply.

"My teacher."

Howard and Evie excused themselves from the table as they scurried into the family room to have a conference. When they returned a few minutes later, Evie laid out the plan. They'd finish their dinner, then they would all help Susan with her assignment.

Vinnie held baby Michael next to Susan and JoBeth as they sat at the table while Evie and Howard took turns being the student and the teacher. A yardstick was used as a pointer for the demonstration.

"Watch closely," Howard urged the children.

Howard, teacher, pointed to Evie, his student, "What does your father do for a living?"

Evie stood up and answered, "Self-employed." Then she sat back down.

"Very good," Howard said.

Next they reversed their roles. Evie pointed to Howard, "What does your father do for a living?"

"Self-employed," he said.

"Very good."

They went through it again, exchanging roles.

"Now you try," Howard pointed at Susan, "What does your father do for a living?"

"He's our dad?" Susan answered.

"No. Self-employed. Say it everyone.

"Self-employed!" Vinnie, Susan, and JoBeth recited, "Self-employed!" Michael clapped his little hands to share in the excitement. But what Evie and Howard had not explained, or demonstrated, was what to say when Mary Bridget, across the aisle, asked another question, "What is self-employed?" Susan answered her with a shrug, "Charlie Brown?" Laughter erupted as the teacher hushed the class and moved on to Walter. "Mechanic," said Walter.

Susan wrapped JoBeth in her arms. JoBeth shook with a fear that Susan could not console as she instructed her, "JoBeth, just do what Mom says. I'll figure something out. I promise." JoBeth found little comfort in Susan's consolation; she knew that Susan was as frightened of Evie as she was. Not one of Evie's children had been able to escape the turmoil she brought into their lives. Evie was a practiced liar and a master rationalizer. This combination of character defects had equipped her to skillfully construct a life of deceit that JoBeth had threatened when she had nodded her head yes. Evie was determined to do everything in her power to suppress the truth, JoBeth's truth. Her priority and intent going forward was to keep the wealth she had so diligently acquired through her relationship with Howard, even if it meant removing JoBeth from the home.

Rosemary was surprised to see Evie at her door. Evie and Rosemary spoke as Susan watched Rosemary's face turn from surprise to concern to worry. Rosemary pushed past Evie and practically ran to the car. She knocked on the window and motioned for Susan and JoBeth to get out. JoBeth could not move, her legs simply did not work. Susan and Rosemary had to hoist JoBeth from the car. Rosemary wrapped her arms around JoBeth's waist and walked her to a bedroom, lay her down like a sleepy child, and put her to bed. Rosemary tucked the covers around JoBeth and said, "Just rest, honey, you can stay here as long as you need."

Rosemary tried to keep her confusion hidden from Susan as she helped Evie unload the suitcases from the car and store them in the hall closet. Rosemary casually offered Susan a cola, like they had just stopped in for a barbecue. Susan politely refused and went outside and sat on the front steps. The summer light faded as she tried to think of what to say to JoBeth. Poor JoBeth. How could she leave her here? Why did she promise to do something for JoBeth when she knew she couldn't? In her heart she knew she would never be able to tell Evie's secrets. And if she ever did find the courage to tell someone, what if no one believed her. This life Evie had created was so complicated and deceitful that even Susan and Vinnie, as they lived it with her, could barely find the words to discuss it. Susan worried too that if Evie was ever caught, she may never see JoBeth or her brothers again. They could disappear, just like her father, Susan thought as she watched a sparrow fly from a branch and land on the precipice of a roof, it calling out sweetly from the steep pitch. Susan rested her head against the cracked yellow door, the sparrow flew off. She closed her eyes and wished for a pair of wings to follow the sparrow into the darkening sky.

JoBeth lay on the bed, her feet curled into her chest. With each breath, the room grew smaller and smaller, so small that JoBeth felt like the wall next to her was just a few inches from her face. The events of the day played over and over again in JoBeth's head. She felt like she was at the movies with the action being far away, not real.

It was laundry day, and she had been doing her chores hastily, while her friend Rebecca waited for her outside. JoBeth climbed the stairs with an armful of laundry to the center hall landing, and dropped them on the bench, where she separated them. One pile to be folded. One pile to be ironed. She folded Vinnie's Fruit of the Looms, Howard's white boxers, and Michael's waffle blanket.

Evie was there on the landing, waiting for her. Her breath was shallow and fast, as she watched JoBeth. Her friend Rebecca had rung the bell too early and woke Evie from her nap. Evie sweated in her purple nylon romper as she stood with her one arm propped on top of the other. Her blue eyes were bloodshot and black eyeliner was caked in the corners. Her bangs curled in the humidity around her bloated cheeks. She finally exhaled loudly, which Evie often did before a tirade. As if her last reasonable breath needed to be expelled from her lungs before she lashed out at whatever irked her at the moment.

"Refold this one, this one, and oh, this one," Evie said. She threw the clothes on the floor. When JoBeth bent over to pick them up, she pushed her down.

"How many times have I showed you how to do this? Fold them again."

JoBeth lay Vinnie's underwear flat, picked up the elastic band at either end, and folded it towards the leg holes, turned it over and folded the left side in first, then the right side. JoBeth set them on the pile on the bench. Evie watched her closely. She scraped an emery board against her long pinky nail which bent from too much pressure. Evie held her hand in the air to examine it, then stuck the tattered nail between her teeth and bit it off. She walked to the bathroom, spit the nail bit into the sink, tossed the emery board into the vanity drawer, and slammed it shut. JoBeth refolded Howard's briefs and the waffle blanket too. Evie continued to watch JoBeth as she said, "After you put them away you can go out to play. Be back for dinner."

"I hate it here. I'm never coming back," JoBeth screamed, a scream that echoed a thousand times over in JoBeth's head.

"What'd you say?" Evie yelled. She picked up the folded clothes and threw them on the floor again, "If you think it's better somewhere else then leave. Go on then, get out!"

Instead JoBeth had run to her room. Susan heard the commotion, scrambled up the stairs and was alarmed to see that JoBeth had pulled her suitcase out of the closet. Susan tried to understand the words that tumbled from JoBeth's mouth. JoBeth was incomprehensible, her small voice apprehensive yet daring to disrupt the sanctuary of silence that Evie imposed on them daily. Evie screamed over JoBeth as Susan pleaded with them both to stop.

"Mom," she cried, "Come, right away. It's an emergency. JoBeth's acting crazy. She's not making sense." Susan, scared now for herself as JoBeth threw open the suitcase, yelled even louder, "Mom, she's packing her things!" Evie entered the room as if she had prepared for this very moment her whole life. She slapped Susan across the face, then turned to JoBeth, held her by the shoulders and violently shook her until she was silent.

JoBeth turned onto her belly, her head rested on her arms. She tried to let go of the feeling of Evie's hands gripping her shoulders flinging her back and forth, back and forth. Then outside her door she heard Rosemary as she questioned Evie. Evie shushed Rosemary as she closed the bedroom door, "I will call you later to check on JoBeth, right now though Susan and I need to get back home before Howard."

Susan and Evie returned home, but JoBeth stayed with Rosemary and Nino. Rosemary moved JoBeth around like another piece of furniture to be swept under as she cleaned the house. She lifted JoBeth up from the couch, over to a chair by the window, then to a kitchen table chair where she would encourage JoBeth to eat. Rosemary served the same peanut butter sandwich over and over again until it was stale and finally she threw it away. Next Rosemary tried canned chicken soup. When it got cold she put it in the fridge. "JoBeth, you'll feel better if you eat something. We'll try again later."

Rosemary talked at JoBeth the whole time and hoped that her constant chatter would comfort JoBeth. Rosemary had called Evie several times and told her she was worried, "Evie, she needs a doctor or a counselor. She hasn't said a word since you left. She's gotta talk — talk to someone." Evie dismissed her assessment of JoBeth and told Rosemary she would return the next day to get JoBeth and that she just needed to get a few more things in order. Rosemary hung up the phone. She had always known Evie was a selfish person but she never imagined that she was capable of choosing a man over her own child — over JoBeth. Yet, that was precisely what she was doing.

Rosemary remembered the day she had first heard about Evie and Howard. Evie had called, chatted for a bit then casually mentioned that she had a new boyfriend. Evie had invited her to come see her new home — he, the boyfriend, had bought her a house. When Rosemary told Nino about the invitation he was reluctant to go. "I don't want to be around her, she's always been trouble," Nino said. Rosemary insisted that they accept the invitation because she was curious; and there was an unspoken jealousy that Rosemary had harbored against Evie since they were children. Evie always seemed to have luck on her side despite the frequent and terrible lies she told. She was the first one to land a husband, the first one to have a baby, and then, the first one to move to the coveted suburban development — Manor Homes. Evie always needed to be first at everything, to win.

Evie casually gave Rosemary directions, "It's on either side of Picturesque Manor and Debutante Parkway. Third on the left, halfway around the cul de sac on Prestige Place. Number 17."

When Rosemary and Nino arrived at Evie's new home there were no words for the level of shock they experienced as Evie gave them a tour of the modern, gray, aluminum-sided, four bedroom house on a double lot. Without any attempt to demonstrate a sense of humility, or even shame, Evie proudly showed them the intercom system, garage door opener, wall-to-wall carpet, dog cages, swimming pool, and a basketball half-court. There was no irony in Evie's voice either as she described how fortunate they were to have chosen the best of all the identical looking houses.

Nino's relentless questions about her new boyfriend finally ceased when Evie sat them down at the kitchen table and asked them to promise to keep a secret. Rosemary felt a sudden wave of affirmation, she knew it, Evie was the other woman and that is why there was no sign of her new boyfriend. Nino was quicker than Rosemary, "Geez, he's married right?" Nino said sharply, barely able to hide his disgust.

"Not quite," Evie whispered, "He's a priest — our priest, Father Howard."

"Father Howard?" Nino and Rosemary said in unison as Rosemary crossed herself.

"He's Father Howard! How can he be your boyfriend?" Nino said as he jumped from the chair, flustered as to what to do next. Rosemary jumped up too, "Evie, this is too much, even for you! What about the children? What about your parents? Do they know?" Rosemary stared at her severely and emanated the closest thing she had ever felt to hate.

"It's not like you think. We fell in love and we are trying to do the right thing for the children, give them a better life," Evie said.

She had told herself this very thing a thousand times since she had moved and yet she wasn't prepared to see Rosemary's and Nino's faces turn from disapproval to disgust. She had expected mercy and compassion; not just for herself, but for Howard too.

"We need to go. We want no part of this," Nino said as he walked towards the door without any attempt to hide his revulsion.

"Where are the children now?" Rosemary asked.

"At my parents, the children know but my parents don't know, yet."

"Well you'll have to tell them at some point. Evie, this just ain't right, no matter what you tell yourself, it ain't right," Rosemary said, as she watched Evie shrug her shoulders and turn away, as she had always done when she was in the wrong. But this time, Rosemary thought, without pity; you will reap what you sow, Evelyn Edwards — yes indeed — you will reap what you sow.

Rosemary approached JoBeth with a tenderness you would give a hurt animal. "Hey sweetie, my little JoBeth, let's get you cleaned up a bit, how about if we wash your hair," Rosemary said as she gently stroked JoBeth's forearm. JoBeth nodded and followed Rosemary to the kitchen sink. Rosemary poured warm water over JoBeth's head, and prayed that God would heal her and keep her safe when she returned home with Evie. Rosemary felt JoBeth's neck soften with each cascade of water. JoBeth had closed her eyes and pretended it was Grandmother Anastasia washing her hair in her old home but was startled back to reality when Rosemary accidentally turned the cold spout on. The cold reminded JoBeth of Howard.

Howard liked his martinis cold. Howard and JoBeth would begin with three ice cubes placed in a bevel-footed glass etched with gold lines and a silver rim. The glass was part of an ornate seven piece set that included a shaker and stirrer. Each glass was three inches high and held four ounces. Howard had them imported from Italy. The vodka and vermouth were kept under the kitchen counter close to the refrigerator. Howard had stocked them there because it was easier for JoBeth to reach.

"Ice first. Then a splash of vermouth, only a splash, not more than a splash, because that is called 'drenched.' Not less than a splash, because that is too dry. Then add the olives," Howard had patiently explained to JoBeth.

JoBeth dropped the cubes in one by one, "Like this?"

"Now, in the US they add the olives last, but to make the proper Italian martini, the olives go in before the vodka."

JoBeth waited while Howard got the olives out of the refrigerator. He grunted as he struggled with the lid and then had taken a knife from the drawer and hit the sides of the silver metal top and said, "See, sometimes you have to break the seal. You try."

JoBeth held the butter knife and tapped the lid, but didn't get it open. Howard told her, "If you ever can't open the jar, just bring it to me. Okay? Got it?"

JoBeth was always eager to get to the vodka, and the shaking parts. The liquor clouded when JoBeth shook it reminding her of a snow globe.

That fogginess, Howard had told her, meant that the ice had broken and would keep his drink colder longer. JoBeth always liked that part, and the next, when she kissed Howard and the bright metallic taste of the vodka glazed her lips.

"Okay, now add the vodka. Just to the second line on the glass. You see that line there?" Howard pointed with his smashed finger. When JoBeth asked him what happened, he replied, "first time bowling."

JoBeth focused on the second line. But she still poured in too much. JoBeth's hand was too small to hold the gallon-sized bottle. After several failed attempts, Howard had a brilliant idea. He poured the vodka into little bottles.

"We'll get a bunch of them like these and fill them up. You'll only have to add one to each drink. Okay? Got it? One little bottle per drink."

JoBeth liked squeezing her hand into the olive jar too. She poked at the slippery green orbs and squished them until the juicy red pimentos fell out. She usually ate three or four while she made Howard his first drink of the evening. As the night wore on, JoBeth mixed drinks and watched television. Sometimes Howard invited her onto the recliner with him and she stayed there, unofficially off duty; Howard encouraging her to take a few sips of his drink. Slightly drunk herself, JoBeth often fell asleep with Howard's arms wrapped around her.

Evie sometimes found them asleep, and then sent JoBeth to bed. In the time *between evening and morning*, Howard often stumbled up the stairs and woke JoBeth with his breath close to her mouth and chest. Some nights Howard laid his head next to JoBeth's on the pillow and whispered drunkenly, "My little martini maker."

When JoBeth made martinis for Howard, she snuck a sip or two. She liked the way the cold vodka stung her lips. She liked vodka so much she snuck the little bottles into her school bag. One day after recess, when JoBeth was in the fourth grade, Sister Martha John pulled her out of line. She had hooked her hands around the back of JoBeth's neck and stuck her big nose close to JoBeth's mouth and sniffed. As she did, the Band-Aid Evie had adhered to JoBeth's neck, that very morning, fell to the ground.

Sister Martha John quickly walked JoBeth to the principal's office. She called Sister Catherine over the intercom. When Sister Catherine entered the office she told JoBeth to empty her pockets. JoBeth did. Out came a crumpled Virginia Slim, a book of matches from Dell's Steakhouse, two small vodka bottles, and a stick of gum, which she had stolen from Evie's purse. These she set down right next to the Pietà figurine, on the principal's desk. Sister Catherine bent down and placed her hands over JoBeth's in a prayer position, and gathered JoBeth's nail-bitten fingers into her own. She stared at the mark just above the collar of JoBeth's blouse. JoBeth knew how it looked, not just a red mark but not quite a bruise.

"What happened to your neck?"

JoBeth said nothing, she kept her eyes on the Pietà.

"Call her mother. Tell her to come to my office immediately," she instructed Sister Martha John.

She asked JoBeth again, "Young lady, who did this to your neck?" JoBeth looked from the Pietà to the blue-eyed, long-haired Jesus portrait that hung crooked on the green cement wall. JoBeth wanted Jesus to tell her what to say.

Sister Catherine snapped open her desk drawer and took out a pen and paper and said, "Write it down. The name of the person who did this to your neck."

JoBeth had thought for a long time. She spelled J-E-S-U-S in her head while Sister paced back and forth behind her. JoBeth wanted Sister to let her go to the spelling bee. She had won last year and gotten the prize, a purple balloon.

Evie strutted into Sister Catherine's office. She wore a bright yellow terrycloth short set with matching high heels. Whiffs of Evie's candy-like perfume and cigarettes and yeasty beer breath infiltrated the room and sent Sister Catherine into a sneezing fit. JoBeth flinched as soon as she saw Evie; her 'don't you dare say a word look' caused JoBeth to drop the pen after she had written the name — Charlie Brown.

Sister Catherine then instructed Evie to follow her into to the hall. It was imperative that they talk — immediately. JoBeth heard Evie mumbling through the closed office door and watched Sister Catherine's head shaking back and forth emphatically as she dismissed Evie's words. Sister Catherine finally ended their conversation and, without lowering her voice, plainly said, "Mrs. Korli, this is a serious situation and your attitude is not helping. I will expect you to address this situation at home and for this never to happen again."

Evie brought JoBeth home as if she were sick and plastered new Band-Aids across her neck. She was sent to her room, where she spent the rest of the day, making Kleenex flowers; enough flowers to cover the entire comforter Susan had helped her sew together from two sheets for a Brownie badge.

Rosemary chatted on about a summer storm that was expected. She dried JoBeth's hair with a towel, gently rubbed the ends with conditioner, then put the purple head band on her. "You look pretty JoBeth. The prettiest girl ever," she said several times throughout the day until Nino got home. Then she was silent like JoBeth.

As promised, Evie returned to pick JoBeth up the next day. They had "bothered" Rosemary long enough. JoBeth clutched her cloth pocket book and Harriet the Spy, still dog-eared on the same page, her hair was combed neatly under her purple head band, as Rosemary helped her into the Cadillac to go home, back to 17 Prestige Place.

Howard waited in the garage for them. He smiled. Such a fuss over a little misunderstanding. JoBeth was fine, wasn't she? Nothing was wrong. Everything was going to be all right. Evie told Howard to leave. "Give us some time, I'll call you later," she said, as Howard backed his army green Cadillac out of the garage. Howard stared at JoBeth, her once clear blue eyes were cloudy and confused. He wanted JoBeth to forgive him, he thought as he started to raise his hand to his forehead to salute her, but the door closed and JoBeth stood there, alone, in the dark garage until Evie returned and retrieved her.

CHAPTER THREE

I n 1956, along First Street, the houses were small, the street was narrow, the windows dark. The homes were sided with gray wood and blended into a long empty streetscape without concern for beauty or aesthetics. A few sheets of newspaper tussled in the wind and hung on the lattice siding of the wooden steps that led to a deep red colored door — the red of the Albanian flag — the door to the Korli's home. A stormy spring rain fell outside as Anastasia boiled the water for her third cup of tea that morning, the nettled soggy leaves, tan instead of brown, sunk to the bottom of the cup, dispensing its light color into the water. Weak tea with a sugar cube was not going to fix the mess her Alek had gotten himself into, but she persisted in drinking and worrying anyway.

The night before, Alek had arrived home and refused his dinner. He tiptoed away to the attic where he had made a room for himself. Anastasia thought that his need to separate himself from the family and move to the attic was a natural demonstration of Alek asserting his independence and manhood. She had not worried, or thought of it again, until she saw his face before he ascended the stairs. It was not the face of a strong man ascending the stairs to his earned room but the face of a scared boy — a guilty boy. Anastasia called Zef from the yard, to come inside right away, something was wrong.

"Has something happened to your brother?"Anastasia asked.

Zef removed his mud boots and brushed dirt from the bottom of his pant leg. He had been tilling the garden he had started last year when his parents bought the house. It was small but large enough to grow the staples for the dishes he loved his mother to cook. He had not appreciated the convenience and careful consideration that went into the plantings of a garden until he was faced with a ten by ten space to grow leeks, peppers, eggplants, cabbage, spinach, and tomatoes. How could he live another year without fresh ingredients for Manti Byrek? And could he add pumpkins to the garden so his mother could make Kungullur again. Anastasia always mashed the pumpkin to just the right consistency then added the butter, salt and sugar, which glazed and burnt the edges of the phyllo dough. Zef longed to smell the baking Kungullur that seeped from the oven into the hospitable, clean kitchen his mother always kept.

Zef remembered when he and Alek had painted the walls of their old kitchen a beautiful green, the color of new leaves. The color was cheerful and elegant, like Anastasia. After she admired their handiwork she had begun her own, and braided rugs from old linens she had torn into long pieces. She placed one of the rugs by the sink and the other under the east facing wall where Alek had painted a tree, using broad thick strokes of a tawny brown paint mixed with dark greens and grays. It was a grand mural that encased a long rectangular window which faced the pasture. A door next to the window led to a small courtyard where the family garden overflowed with vegetables and spices.

Back home in Korce, Zef and George had competed to grow the sweetest tomato or largest head of cabbage. Anastasia and Alek were the judges and their neighbor Droika would intervene if there wasn't consensus. Now Droika, the old garden, the large heads of cabbage cleaned and chopped on his mother's cutting board as she prepared their dinner; it was all so far away. And here they were now, new immigrants in a new home, and she, his dear mother having to ask if anything was wrong with Alek, his older brother.

It was inexcusable what Alek had done. How could he tell his mother that his older brother had brought shame to the family and be the first to witness her discovery of Alek's deed? Her eldest son's deplorable behavior will break her heart. He had warned Alek that his actions were indefensible and had grave concerns for both him and Evie. He went so far as to apologize for flirting with the two American sisters in the first place. He also implored Alek to stop seeing Evie. What kind of girl meets a boy in the park alone? He warned Alek that Evie Edwards was not their kind and although there were some men who were permitted to sow their oats before marriage, their parents' reputation could be put at risk, especially their mother's, if it was even suggested she had raised such men. What consequences would they all endure for the sake of his proclaimed love for an American girl? Alek refused to heed Zef's imploring and accused him of being Old World, and after one heated exchange even called him a jackass.

"Zef, don't ignore me. What has happened to Alek?" Anastasia had lost her patience with Zef's procrastination, his slow untying of his boots, his sweeping and swatting at his pant legs.

"Nene, please, don't ask me. Ask Alek."

"I am asking you, my youngest son to tell me of his brother," Anastasia's eyes darted away to let him know she was serious about listening.

"As your son, and as Alek's brother, you must hear from him Nene, please."

Zef knew that he was invoking the idea of Gjakmarrja, a blood feud, and in doing so prevented her from further inquiry, since even a suggestion of blood-taking was only discussed among men. This caused Zef much pain and sorrow to do this to his mother but the alternative was the same. Anastasia understood that the news must be quite terrible for Zef to try to distract and quiet her with a mysterious, and unlikely threat of Gjakmarrja. Zef was relieved when she looked him in the eye and reached over to stroke his shoulder, "You are a good brother and a good son, my young one," she said with a heavy sigh, "my Zef."

As George walked home from his work at the steam engine factory, he always looked forward to entering the door to his home, his American home. However this evening, Anastasia sat on the steps and wrung her hands in dismay, her expression was one George had only seen once before and that was when she had to tell him his mother had passed. Anastasia jumped up from the step when she saw George and rushed toward him and urged him to come quickly. Something was wrong with Alek.

The Korlis' had acquired their American home after careful and shrewd negotiations that were mediated by a close neighbor and friend of the family. The bargaining started after a neighbor, Sophie, mentioned to Anastasia that she heard the house next to her was to be put up for sale. A Greek family was selling it and was planning to move to Boston. Anastasia solicited the help of Sophie's son, Dritan, who was friends with the Greek neighbor's son, Arnos. Without asking George, Anastasia printed in Greek on a piece of paper, 'how much do I need to buy your house?' She folded the slip of paper and gave it to Dritan to bring to Arnos's home to give to his mother, which he did and promptly returned with the same piece of paper.

Anastasia's swallowed loudly when she unfolded the paper and looked at the price carefully written, the numbers printed so large they practically jumped off the page. She wrote her counteroffer on a new slip of paper. She gave the note to Dritan, who gave it to Arnos, who gave it to his mother and again the note was promptly returned with another counteroffer. This persisted, the two boys running notes between the women, until, finally the price and purchase arrangements were agreed upon with the women's pride remaining intact. It was then that Anastasia finally told George that she had purchased a home for the family.

George heard the words come from Anastasia's mouth but his ears defied them.

"I dashur Grua, my dear, dear wife, I hear your words but don't understand," George said, looking over her shoulder to show he was ready to listen, concentrate on her words.

"Une bleu shtepi," Anastasia said.

She did not look at George directly to show her respect and love.

"Zemra ime, my sweetheart, again, I hear you but don't understand. How did you buy a house?"

George was beyond disbelief and comprehension. Where would the money for a house come from? He knew that Anastasia had been sending money to her brother, Ektor, and his family, in Turkey. Ektor had left Albania to work, but was unprepared when Turkey started to turn on its migrant workers. It came as quite a surprise that such extreme hatred had grown unbeknownst to Ektor and his wife, Katina, especially after such a long and welcomed respite of good wages and excellent schools for the children. They had even hung a Turkish flag from their apartment window.

Ektor and his family had hidden in a basement for three weeks during a pogrom, until a kind and loyal Turkish family helped them buy passage to Belgium. The slaughter of Albanians, Jews, and Greeks during the pogrom rendered Ektor mute. Katina, wrote long despondent letters to Anastasia about her brother's mental condition. Ektor had confessed to Katina, in a flurry of emotion and distress, that he had planned to kill her and their four daughters if the Turks invaded the home where they were hidden. Ever since he revealed this honorable, yet horrific thought to his wife, he had not spoken another word.

Anastasia had begun sending Katina money immediately. Not even a bar of soap for the family was bought until the last bits of the old bar had disintegrated into the drain. Anastasia was only one year older than Ecktor but she felt as if he were her twin. If he felt pain, she felt pain. To have acquired a house with the financial stress they had all endured, fortunate as it was, but still a burden, was just unfathomable, even to George who was always impressed with Anastasia's call to sacrifice, her willingness to help others, and her allegiance to uphold Besa in the family. Her dedication to live honestly and truthfully, and to sacrifice her comfort and her family's comfort for what was right and just was why he loved her, and her demonstration of those values exuded a spiritual beauty that surpassed the physical beauty that many men often desired in their wives.

His love for her was utmost when she was in action, engaged, not distant from him, but not too close, and this is when sudden desire struck him like a school boy. The deep gut longing to hold her close, love her tenderly, and make her laugh, were accessible feelings that presented themselves often and mysteriously. George loved Anastasia and she loved him, and never, since their first understanding that their parents had engaged them at birth, had they questioned the other's love and dedication to building a good family, a strong family, a family that upholds the promise of all the good that comes from Besa. She was a good wife, and he was a good husband, and they were blessed with two good sons.

Because Anastasia knew of George's weakness for card playing, a habit he had acquired in his teens, she did not tell him the exact amount of money she had made at the Saturday market in Korce selling bridal wear and textiles that were usually given to brides after their betrothal. Often alone at night, after George left to see "if kesmet was on my side that night," Anastasia had honed a signature style. Many brides desired her items and traveled from faraway villages to buy them. A popular piece was a beaded veil, woven with flat gold discs that looked like coins. She also made all the pieces of the traditional wedding clothing men wore, including a Qeleshe, which matched the popular bridal veil, with one strand of beads and a single gold disc that swung from the tip of the hat. Anastasia learned too that the further the women traveled to buy her goods, the more they would pay. The extra money made from faraway clients, she hid from George.

Before they had boarded the ship to come to America, Anastasia fretted night and day about how she would transport the bundles of lek she had saved. One morning she woke with the idea to sew a skirt with hidden pockets and two hems. At the market, her table happened to be near a woman who sold plastikos, film-like sheets. The crinkled sheets of plastic were considered a luxury and a desired item by the locals since they could be used to wrap food and were used as liners around baby diapers. Anastasia traded the woman a few embroidered doilies for five large sheets of plastic. She carefully wrapped small piles of leks in the clear sheets before she wrapped them again in a cotton packet and then sewed the packets into the skirt. After they arrived in America she only took the skirt off to bathe, and to be with George, but even then, it never left her sight.

After they arrived in Albany, she demanded the family live frugally to increase their chances of survival, and to uphold her commitment to helping her brother come to America. When it had been time to purchase the house, Anastasia called on Alek to go to the bank with her, but he refused. He confessed that his English was still too poor to discuss finances with a bank teller. This was the first time "I will kill you," had slipped from Anastasia's mouth. Although it was common for Albanian parents to say this to their children, she and George had decided to refrain from this habit that so many new parents fell into. Alek was startled by his mother's words, so much so that he almost cried in front of her. This was when Alek went to Zef and told him that he must go to the bank with their mother and accepted the humiliation of needing to call on his younger brother for help.

Anastasia relayed all this to George whose shame had risen from the bottom of his heart and pressed tears from his eyes, a stream of ignominy drenched his reddened face. How had he let his affinity for gambling usurp his responsibilities to provide a good and decent home for his family? How could he have squandered even a penny away from his loving wife and good sons? George's mortification brought him to the feet of his wife, surrendering to his remorse and need for redemption. Anastasia with grace and love, knelt beside him and embraced her shaken husband and dried the bitter tears of George's self reproach.

"You are my good luck, why was I looking somewhere else for it?" George said, determined to show Anastasia that his remorse was sincere and not temporary. Anastasia rose and pulled George up with her, she stood before him, reached in her pocket, and pulled out a brass key with a cardboard tag with Korli printed on it. She pressed the key into George's hand, kissed each of his fingers tenderly, and then held his gaze like a new bride. He, in turn, reached into his pocket, and, without compunction, offered his wife the money he had won at the last game of cards he was to ever play during his lifetime.

George climbed the steep steps to the attic, while Anastasia and Zef huddled at the bottom step to listen in. George shooed them away and they reluctantly took two steps backward. George found Alek with his face buried in his pillow, his fist punched at the mattress with such force that feathers flew in every direction.

"Alek? Alek!" George called from the top step, his breath shortened by the climb. Alek turned toward the wall and covered his face. George had never seen his boy cry, nor would he encourage it.

"Alek, come down for dinner," George demanded. He waited by the door for Alek to obey.

"Baba, I have to tell you something," Alek said. He smoothed the pillow and stood to face his father. George stolidly crossed his arms at his chest and nodded for Alek to continue.

"I need to get married."

"Why do you need to marry?"

"I will have my own family soon."

"Is it that American girl you have been hiding from us?" George asked, but already knew his son would nod his head yes.

"Evie. Her name is Evie."

"How old is this Evie?"

"Seventeen. Older than when you and Nene married."

"She may be older in age, but not heart. This is not the same. What will her parents expect from us?"

"I think just to marry her, it's not like the old country Baba."

"Things are never that simple, Alek," George said. He narrowed his eyes to meet Alek's, "Do you think she will make a good wife?"

Alek looked in his father's eyes for a long moment.

"Yes, I do love her," Alek said and ignited a fear in George when he saw a faint relief that warmed the cool green pools of Alek's eyes. How had his oldest son become a lost romantic? Who was this American girl who weakened his son's sense of honor and duty to his family?

"I should tell your mother. It should be me, not you," George said. He descended the stairs to eat his cold supper.

When George broke the news to Anastasia she wept as if Alek had died. What had she done wrong she asked George repeatedly as she rocked and sobbed at the kitchen table. Her plate untouched, her bare feet slid back and forth across the tile floor. Who was this devil girl who had trapped her son? What did Alek know about love? How would he finish school? Did he even know where she went to church? Would the child be raised Orthodox? Would they be allowed to name the child? Anastasia's questions finally subsided late in the evening when there was not another tear to fall or doubt to be reassured. She fell asleep, her head resting in the crook of her arm on the kitchen table, her feet twisted into her long skirt for warmth. George retrieved an afghan from the couch and covered her shoulders, unpinned her long black braid from her head, and loosened it at the nape of her neck, just as Anastasia had done herself each night of their marriage before she lay her head on his chest.

George shuffled towards bed and turned down the lights as he went. He didn't bother to light the bedside lamp as he put on his sleeping pants. The streetlight lit the window enough for him to hang his shirt, fold his trousers, and place his watch on the bureau. He left the door ajar for Anastasia. George lay alone in their bed. The house seemed bigger than it really was, the news of a baby, his grandchild, filled the empty space where Anastasia would have slept. When a new sun peeked up from the horizon, George made the sign of the cross, but could not pray. His wish for peace was interrupted by the sounds of stifled weeping coming from the attic floor which made George feel blood-sick, the kind of sickness that was transferred between kin, specifically between males. Sometimes it was an old feud that rumbled through a man's veins. Other men suffered from the flow of new dishonors and became stewards of their family's failures. George prayed that it was just a passing feeling, he knew many poor men who never recovered. The legacy of their blood sickness and buried anguish provoked constant nausea and unease. George sat up suddenly, aware of the squeaking door, the creaking steps, the sound of Alek's footsteps as he crept down the hall like a thief, and snuck out of the house to avoid his mother.

When Anastasia woke her face was dry and tight, as if all the salt from her body had been expelled from her cheeks and jaw. The knuckles on her hand pulsed and burned. The stress and unsettled sleep had caused a flare up of arthritis. The approaching daylight did not make things better as George had promised. Anastasia lit the stove and warmed her hands as her eyes fixed on a small picture of Korce her father had painted and had hung in her mother's kitchen. She was proud to hang the painting in her American kitchen, her sunny pleasant kitchen, now silenced and sallow with the news of a grandchild. She felt Alek's situation was even more hopeless than it was the night before.

A new flood of questions would need to be answered she realized with dismay. Where will Alek and Evie live? Will Evie live with her, as is tradition? How would she teach an American to care for an infant? Could she help raise a child at the age of fifty-eight? If Evie did move in, which chores would she take over? Does she even know how to cook for Albanian men? Does she understand the Kunan and a woman's responsibilities in the home? The question that surfaced most was how could Alek disregard their tradition of marriage and family? She wondered if George was secretly angry with her for failing as a mother. Or did he hold himself responsible for Alek's allegiance to a foreigner and not seeking a proper arrangement for his son? What kind of people are Welsh people anyway? Anastasia knew little of the rest of Europe and was suspicious of strangers as a general rule. She realized that if the situation was reversed, and it was Evie's parents that had a son and had to take on an Albanian daughter, that they too might be conflicted and sorrowed. How does one marry an outsider? It had never crossed her mind that she would ever be confronted with this question.

In her mind, George would have recognized that Alek was ready to marry, and he would have written to a good family in Korce to learn the status of a daughter similar in age to Alek and worthy of a dowry. The families would have bickered over, then negotiated the dowry until stones were moved from a roadway to give the family left behind access to do business in another village, or the price of a herd of goats was deemed reasonable. This barter would continue until a level of equanimity was felt by the father of the bride and the father of the groom. Never, ever, did she imagine that she would wonder what religion her grandchild would be. She hoped that they were at least Catholic and not Protestant. In her heart she knew that the only way to survive this was to surrender. Completely. She would welcome her grandchild and abide by her duty to raise an Orthodox, law abiding, loving child of God.

CHAPTER FOUR

A few months later Anastasia brought a heaping basket of vegetables and dried flowers to her friend Sophie. She wanted to offer thanks for Sophie's help in purchasing the Korli home and ask her to attend a dinner she planned for Alek and Evie. She had invited Evie and her parents, Will and Doris, to her home to formally acknowledge the union of their children. George was suspicious of Alek's understanding that Evie's family expected nothing from the Korlis, not a dowry of any kind seemed inexplicable. What kind of family gives their daughter away to strangers?

Anastasia was taken aback, and somewhat remorseful, after she had reached out to Sophie who had made it clear that she was averse to celebrating a grandchild conceived outside of marriage.

"I admire your piety Sophie, but this is my grandchild and you are my only friend here. So please come — you must come," Anastasia said.

She swept the dirt from Sophie's stoop with her hand.

"Stop that, this minute, I'll get a broom," Sophie said, reaching into the hallway to get the broom. Anastasia continued to sweep away the dirt with her hands anyway. How could she make Sophie understand that this bond between Alek and Evie will not be broken and if she tried to break it, the bond would strengthen? Alek was stubborn that way. She needed Sophie to help her face Evie's parents, to show them that the Korlis' were not here alone, that they could not be taken advantage of; that they were part of a community.

"All done," Anastasia said.

"Of course you are, always have to have things your way."

"Not always, but please come Sophie, we are afraid to face them on our own. What if they don't like us? And then we may never see our grandchild."

"They are Welsh people, not monsters Anastasia. You worry too much."

Anastasia took the broom and swept over where she already swept to show Sophie she was staying until she agreed.

"Okay, okay, stop sweeping for goodness sakes. I will come early and help with the cooking and then stay until it is time for dinner." Anastasia handed Sophie the broom. Hugged her tightly then stroked her forearm, "Thank you my dear friend, thank you."

A few days later Sophie was at the door. She juggled a baking sheet full of baklava, a moussaka casserole, stuffed grape leaves, and a bottle of homemade wine.

"What's all this?" Anastasia exclaimed, surprised that her friend not only kept her word but had brought so many gifts.

"It's nothing. Help me here."

"Thank you Sophie, thank you," Anastasia said.

The smell of roasted lamb and mint from the warm casserole filled the room.

"You're a grandmother now. A gjyshe! We'll show those Welsh folks how we Albanian women cook!"Anastasia set down the casserole and helped Sophie unload the rest of the dishes.

"They will love this Sophie. I was just frying some haloumi and washing grapes from the yard. With all this, the only thing left to do is make pita."

Sophie smiled and pulled four loaves of fresh pita from her shoulder bag. Anastasia began to cry and stroked Sophie's forearm. How did she ever come to deserve such a good friend, a loyal friend?

"And wine too!"Anastasia exclaimed to relay her gratefulness.

"That's for us! I thought you may need a small glass to settle your nerves."

Anastasia took two empty jelly jars from the cupboard while Sophie uncorked the bottle. "That Evie will keep you drinking for a long time to come," Sophie jested.

Sophie was referring to that time when Alek had told them of Evie's pregnancy. Anastasia had insisted Alek bring Evie to their home so they could meet her. Alek resisted at first and made excuses. He was too busy with school. Evie wasn't feeling well. This went on for a few weeks until Alek relented and agreed to bring Evie home for dinner. Anastasia had called Sophie shortly after Evie had arrived. Evie hadn't been in their home for more then five minutes before she settled herself on Alek's lap at Anastasia's kitchen table. Mortified that a young woman, an obviously pregnant girl nonetheless, was sitting on her son's lap in her very own kitchen, Anastasia had snuck away and called Sophie. George had cleared his throat then excused himself saying that he needed to check on something. Alek, Evie and Zef remained at the table. Zef tried to follow his father but George insisted he stay with Alek and Evie.

"Sophie, come right away, I have never seen such a thing," Anastasia whispered into the phone. Sophie had hurried over expecting to find some kind of medical emergency, and was surprised as well that there was, in fact, an American girl sitting on Alek's lap at the family table. Sophie and Anastasia stood on the stoop, Sophie tried her best to console Anastasia. "She will learn, it will take time," Sophie repeated until Anastasia and George had the courage and patience to finish their introduction to Evie.

"Say when," Sophie said, pouring the fragrant sweet juice into Anastasia's jar.

"When, when, when, when!" Anastasia laughed, and raised the full jar into the air, "Shëndeti tuaj, to your health!"

"Shëndeti tuaj," Sophie raised her jar to Anastasia, then the two women threw their heads back and finished their wine in one gulp.

"Now you are ready for anything! Even lap sitting," Sophie laughed.

"One can only hope, one can only hope," Anastasia said tenderly.

At half past six the doorbell rang. Evie, Doris, and Will Edwards stood on the top step of the stoop. Will had wanted to walk over but Doris insisted they drive because Evie was nine months pregnant and shouldn't be on her feet that long. Evie was worried that the Welsh cakes her mother had made were too much like a breakfast food and had wanted her to make caramel squares instead, but Doris insisted on bringing the most traditional dish she knew, and even used bacon fat instead of butter, which made Evie's already queasy stomach even more so.

George, Alek and Zef arrived at the door at the same time. Alek nudged Zef out of the way as George opened it and greeted the Edwards. Anastasia and Sophie were not far behind, each untying their aprons as they got nearer to their guests.

"Welcome. Welcome to our home," George said, as Alek, Anastasia, and Sophie all nodded and smiled their best smiles.

"Thank you for coming!" Anastasia said in her best English.

"Of course, we have been looking forward to meeting you both," Will said and removed his hat before he stepped through the doorway. Doris and Evie smiled and followed.

Anastasia took Will's hat and hung it on the coat rack as Sophie took the Welsh cakes from Evie and brought them to the kitchen. When she returned, George was just finishing introductions.

"And this is our dear friend from church, Sophie."

"Pleased to meet you," Doris said.

The families stood in the foyer not quite sure what to do next. Sophie flitted about and patted seats indicating to their guests to sit. Doris and Will sat on the sofa, Alek and Evie sat on the radiator covers. Sophie brought in two dining chairs for George and Anastasia.

"It is so nice of you to invite us," Doris said.

She unbuttoned her sweater. For a November evening the room was quite warm but smelled good of roasting meats and baked dough of some sort. She was surprised at how short Alek's parent's were. The father had a big knob at the end of his nose that made him look a bit like WC Fields. His pants were baggy around the thighs and his shoes were quite scuffed. The mother looked like a peasant with her braided hair and long skirts. She was wearing men's corduroy slippers with white sports socks of all things.

"Our English is not so good so excuse me," Anastasia said, and she gestured at George to include him. She slid her feet back and forth nervously as she smoothed the doily on the back of George's chair.

"Oh it is quite fine, surprisingly fine given you have only been here a short while," said Will and wondered when they would be offered something to drink.

"Thank you. That is good to hear," said George as he patted Anastasia on the knee.

"It's always hard the first few years. Even though we heard English back home, it was still difficult to get the hang of it."

"When did you come here?" George asked.

"Back in '18. Right after the first war," Will replied.

"Ah that was a bad one. '40 was bad too in Albania."

"40 we were here, that was the year Evie was born."

"Alek too."

Alek and Evie looked at one another, this was going much better than they expected.

"Ana may I help you with something in the kitchen?" Doris asked.

"Thank you, all okay," Anastasia said, looking to Alek to be sure she had responded correctly in English. Alek shook his head once to acknowledge she had been understood by all.

Sophie brought in a tray of grape leaves, jars filled with water, and two jars filled with wine for the men. George handed Will a jar of wine, each man raised their jar, George called out first, "To our grandchild!"

Then Will, clinked his jar to George's jar, "To our grandchild!"

Alek and Evie smiled at one another. Doris and Anastasia shared a moment of relief as the two men drank their wine.

"Alek and I have chosen names. Susan if it is a girl, and Vincent if it is a boy," Evie said as she swung her arm around Alek's shoulder.

"Evie not now, like I told you before, we have to wait until after the baby is born," Alek said to his father, and hoped to appease him by adding, "We will all decide then."

"Those are nice names," Doris said, turning toward Will with a slightly confused look, "Aren't they Will?" Will shrugged in agreement but was aware of a growing tension in the room.

"Susan? Vincent?" Anastasia repeated and looked to Alek, "What is this Susan and Vincent names, your father is supposed to —?"

"It can wait Ana, like Alek said," George interrupted and raised his glass again, "to our grandchild."

Will raised his glass again but it was empty. Alek refilled it and after an awkward moment, Will toasted George one more time. George was impressed with Will's height and hoped that a future of taller Korlis would be a benefit of this intermarriage. And more physical beauty in the family could result as well; Will's wife had produced an attractive, well-proportioned daughter that had her blues eyes, good teeth, and light hair. His future grandchild, George thought, could inherit height and the best features of the Albanians and Welsh. An image of a smiling, lanky, olive-skinned, blond-haired, blue-eyed boy formed in his mind that reminded him of the Ancient Greeks.

When Sophie entered the room and called everyone to dinner, Anastasia rose a bit too quickly as she tried to hide her anger at Alek. How could Alek have let Evie disrespect his father in his own home? Susan and Vincent were not names that George would have chosen for his first grandchild. He had promised her that if it was a boy he would name it Ektor after her brother, and if it was a girl it was to be named after his mother, Lule, which meant beautiful flower.

Evie's parents, Doris and Will Edwards, had settled in West Hills just one street from the Italian neighborhood which had slowly edged out the Irish; sending those with surnames like McGeary and Murphy deeper into the black neighborhoods. Their neighbor, Mrs. Grimaldi, used a washboard in the yard, and tried her best to converse with them as she hung or removed laundry from the line. Doris took kindly to Mrs. Grimaldi, her first friend after leaving her family's rooming house in a leather-stocking town in Upstate New York.

On Wednesday afternoons, when Mrs. Grimaldi returned from the Italian market she would invite Doris over for a cup of espresso. Doris disliked the bitterness of the freshly ground beans, but the petite cups and saucers with painted scenes of famous Italian landmarks made it tolerable to down the strong coffee in one sip. Her heart would race for a minute until she took a bite of the homemade biscotti Mrs. Grimaldi set aside for their visits.

At sixteen, Doris had met Will, a tall, thin Welshman. She thought he was handsome, and often commented that, "we wore the carpet out between our bedrooms." Will had come to the States at fourteen under the charge of his brother Thomas who was eighteen. They left St. David's, a small town on the River Alun, on a dreary spring day after their parents, Meneva and Edwin, had died in a house fire.

Two days before Christmas, Thomas and Will returned from the forest to find the house ablaze. They had been dragging a large pine from the forest, intended to hold the ginger cookies and felt stockings their mother had made, when they discovered their father's body. Edwin had crawled outside, most likely to try to save the bee yard. He was alive momentarily until he relented and took his last breath from his burnt lungs. They found their mother, near the stove with an empty bucket in her hand. The confused bees buzzed around the brothers as they held one another and watched the fire burn until their beloved home was buried under a dense bed of cinder and ashes.

St. David's was a small town, poor, and favored for taking care of its own. The boys were immediately surrounded by distant kin and neighbors; the closest of neighbors watched over them as they grieved and buried their parents. The area around the town was known as Meneva, which was their mother's name as well. Will and Thomas loved to say her name, sometimes calling her Mama Meneva. When they did, a look of contentment flushed her face for a moment before she gently reprimanded them to call her Mother. The formalities of the monastery that St. David founded were etched into the manners of the townspeople. Family members were always called by their kinship roles, Mother, Father, Brother, and Sister.

The Edwards were known in town for their apiculture skills. Their Uncle Milton and their father, Edwin, were master apiarists and their mother had learned to preserve the royal jelly and made honey-colored candles with the beeswax. She sold them at the Saturday market. The bee yard held several hundred hives and was visited each spring by farmers far and near to buy the famous Edwards bees to pollinate their crops.

Thomas and Will were sad to leave their poor village, the loneliness each suppressed was channeled into the details of their departure as they planned their trip to America. A neighbor had given them two small leather trunks. They packed and repacked the trunks in the evenings by the last light of the flickering lantern. Should they take the extra woolen socks Mrs. Jones had made for them? Should they just wear two sets of their clothes and take one trunk? They were certain they would bring the cross that had hung over the front door of their home. It was one of the few objects their father had held dear. He often remarked that 'less is more' as he reflected on its simple ornamentation. Their father often quoted Browning and spent many evenings quietly reciting poems or dramatic monologues while Meneva and the boys drifted to sleep. The cross was also dear to Will because it had hung over the door of his mother's and grandmother's home and was given to Meneva on their wedding day. The silver cross, charred and in need of polishing, was rolled in their mother's handkerchief and then a tea towel that had been left outside to dry the day of the fire. The boys created a false bottom in the trunk to put extra coins, the cross, and paper rubbings of their parent's gravestones. As the ship left port, the brothers squinted under a strong sun to see their village one last time, to imprint its buildings and people on their hearts. The brothers returned to Meneva only during their dreams, which they never wanted to wake from.

Their Uncle Milton had moved to the States ten years earlier after the boys had grown to an age when they could help their father in the bee yard. As they walked to the river port to board the boat to America they looked like lumber jacks dressed in two sets of clothes, their hands, wrapped in Mrs. Jones's big wooly socks. Will and Thomas gripped the iron handle of the one steamer trunk that contained all their belongings as they detoured past the magnificent cathedral and the well-kept clergy homes to bid farewell to their hometown.

Uncle Milton had landed a job working on the railroad in the West Hills of Albany as part of the section crew responsible for track maintenance. He asked the foreman to hire Thomas and Will. Having only one spot available the brothers flipped a coin and Will began work as a lineman. His job was to unload the freight cars when they arrived at the station. Will's youth, his kind voice, and his equally defined soft accent, made him vulnerable to the harder men who worked the rail. They chided him for keeping the breast pocket of his starched uniform filled with caramels and butterscotches. His Welsh accent and sweet tooth were seen as a weaknesses, as feminine, in the musty dank rail yard where men sweated and cursed and anticipated the day's end when a cold beer and a thin cabbage stew awaited them at home.

When dinner was over the two fathers, Will and George, stood at the front door, shook hands, and agreed that the families were adequately prepared for their soon-to-be-born grandchild. The two mothers exchanged recipes, even though neither would ever attempt to make the other's dish. Alek asked everyone to wait for just a moment; he turned to Zef who handed him a small red velvet box. Alek set down on one knee and proposed to Evie. She quickly accepted the ring and kissed Alek on the cheek. After Alek rose to his feet, George and Will patted him on the back and assured him he would make a good father and husband. Evie held her hand in the air for her mother and Anastasia to admire the silver band set with a glass stone. There was a long silent moment and Zef couldn't think of a thing to say. He was not happy for his brother or for his future niece or nephew. Zef excused himself to help Sophie with the dishes.

"Before marriage we open our eyes wide, after marriage we tighten them," Sophie said as she handed the bottle of wine to Zef. He took a long swig as Sophie held out her glass. "Say when," Zef teased. 'When, when, when," Sophie repeated and grinned as she accepted the generous pour, leaned towards Zef and clinked her glass against the bottle. Sophie patted Zef's cheek gently and whispered, "Don't worry so much Zef. Everything will turn out the way it is meant to be."

Will, Doris, and Evie drove home. The evening clouds hung low as the first pangs of labor rose and fell in Evie's belly.

CHAPTER FIVE

1968

At Dell's Steakhouse, Evie hauled a tray into the kitchen. She swung her hip and pushed open the door. A sharp edge on the kick panel snagged her nylon as she rushed to get the phone. Max, the cook, answered, scowled, and without saying anything handed the receiver to Evie.

"Hello?" Evie said as she pulled clear nail polish from her apron pocket and dabbed at the new hole.

"Okay. I said okay! I'll be there in ten minutes," Evie said, fumbling with the receiver as she tried to hang it up, not because she hadn't known what the call was about but because Max had stopped scowling at her and winked. Maybe Max wasn't so mean after all Evie thought as she headed to Stan's office.

Stan had heard the phone slam and the tap tap of Evie's heels on the linoleum floor as she rushed toward the office. He tried to close the door before she got to it. Evie was quicker, pushed the door open, and threw her arm up against the jamb revealing the edging of a red bra.

"Not so fast."

Stan sat at his desk and pretended to pencil something in his ledger.

"Stan. I gotta go. It's Vinnie again."

"No Evie. You just got here. And it's almost lunch hour."

"I'll be back in twenty minutes. It's slow now."

Stan hated that he was easily distracted by these uncomfortable little thoughts about Evie. The image of the red bra would haunt him the rest of the day, into the night, and then become a long, dark dream he wouldn't shake for days.

"It'll take you twenty to get there," Stan said, mustering a tone of civility to hide his disdain for being managed by the help. Evie bowed her head to acknowledge Stan's disapproval.

"Back in thirty minutes or don't bother," Stan said, without hesitation.

"Thanks Stan. I owe you," Evie said, wrinkled her nose, and then added, "I'll slap the little bastard once for you."

Evie turned to leave, but before she did, she swayed her hips just a bit for Stan. He shook his head, closed his eyes as if crestfallen, and returned to penciling numbers into his ledger; just as he had done for the past twenty years.

Dell's Steakhouse was the only thing his father left him. Eighty tables, two bars, a large hall for proms and weddings, a coat room, four bathrooms, one large kitchen, and twelve aging waitresses. His father, Big Jack, as the employees were told to call him, paid well, kept the place clean, and treated everyone like family. Edna, his first wife, left when she discovered he was having an affair with Charlene, one of the younger waitresses, Stan's mother. Stan had inherited her slight frame, puffy eye sacks, and bristly blond hair.

Stan, like his father, had tried his hand at bartending, cooking, and even host, but when he opened the ledgers, he finally found his place at Dell's. He also now understood that Big Jack wasn't just a penny pincher, a cheapskate; he had been a careful man, a meticulous man. He had demonstrated his love for order and precision in the care that he took to document every transaction and every minute he had spent running the banquet house.

Stan had learned early on to never ask his father for anything. Big Jack expected any son of his to earn his own way, and often commented to Stan when he had lingered at a candy counter, or peered in the toy store window on the way to the bank, "A man's self-worth comes from how much he is worth. Make money, save money, then decide what it is you really want." And like his father, the numbers, the simplicity of making things balance each and every night, had become Stan's evening prayers.

After Big Jack died, and the older waitresses quit because their backs and feet gave out, Stan exclusively hired young pretty woman who were too busy flirting for tips to notice him. He had found contentment left alone in the office with his books. The only exception to his need for solitude was his secret longing to see Evie at least once during her shift. He pretended otherwise, but he knew that Evie understood the boundaries he had set for their relationship and she never crossed them. Even though she was trouble right from the start and turned out to be a decent liar, Stan recognized immediately that Evie's aptitude for spinning tales was also her strength.

Being a good liar was the key to success in the restaurant business. If customers believed that you actually liked them, then an acceptable, and sometimes even a generous tip, was guaranteed. Waitstaff who succeeded understood that the fundamental need of a customer was to be liked and applied the proper level of obsequiousness to make them feel welcomed and adored. Waitstaff who failed to ingratiate themselves to the customers often failed then quit, or Big Jack fired them.

Stan was also very aware that his feelings for Evie were conflicted. Evie reminded him of his own mother by the way she bit her bottom lip, bent her head toward her chest and tucked a loose strand of hair behind her ear before she spoke. He enjoyed her little dramas and watching her twist and turn any small detail in a story to benefit herself. He was amused by how the other woman hated her and Evie's defiant stare when she passed them by. Her beauty was unmatched and there was not a person alive who would take one look at her body and believe Evie Edwards had four children waiting for her at home.

Evie popped her head in the kitchen and whispered to Max, "Be back soon, promise," she said. Max chopped an onion in half, looked up at Evie with a smirk and said, "Sure thing. And tell that boy of yours to knock it off or I'll be going to pick him up next time."

"Thanks Max, I appreciate you and Stan being so understanding and all," Evie said. She grabbed her purse from the coat hook and hurried out the door.

Evie blessed herself as she got into the old Plymouth. A new ritual since the white Valiant had been getting stuck in reverse lately. Her father, Will, had purchased the car for her after she had left Alek. Will worried that something terrible would happen to Evie walking home from the bus stop after her evening shift. And, he knew she urgently needed a car to go to the market with the children.

One summer afternoon, Evie had called Will to come get her and the children after the grocery bag Vinnie carried broke. In the wretched heat, Evie struggled to manage the four children, pick up the strewn groceries across the sidewalk, and tried to avoid becoming a spectacle. Michael had begun to cry. JoBeth had thrown herself on the ground and refused to walk another step while Susan and Vinnie argued over who was going to have carry her home. A few passersby had stopped and asked if Evie needed help, which made Evie feel even more self-conscious, as if she had done something wrong. Will had arrived a half hour later to find the five of them leaned against the Woolworth's storefront in the hot sun. Their extraordinary closeness was wrapped in a kind of despair that broke his heart. Will had packed the trunk with the bags while Evie herded the children into the car. He drove them home without saying a word. The next day Will had appeared at the flat, keys dangled from a new leather ring. This gift from her father was more than Evie had ever expected. She had disappointed Will so many times, yet, still, he would not be deterred from being the father, the kind-hearted man, that he was.

Evie prayed it wouldn't take thirty minutes just to get out of the parking lot. She pushed the reverse button and backed up. It was stuck. She backed up as far as she could, stopped, and banged her head several times on the steering wheel. After a moment she rested her head on the wheel, and pressed the cool, hard vinyl into her forehead until she calmed down. In these kinds of situations Evie felt as if everything was against her. She desperately wanted someone to rescue her from herself; to come along and remake her life into the one she had wished for, the one she thought she deserved. She laid her head back on the headrest and felt even emptier.

Evie thought of Vinnie and all that he had been through in his eleven years. His inescapable destiny was sorrowfully bound in his birth to a naive mother, and a reluctant father. Everyday life was a struggle as it pertained to how to run a household and raise a child. She knew that what lay at the heart of her relationship with Vinnie's father was simply that she didn't like the Albanian boy she fell in love with after he had become a man, and then a father. She thought of the unspoken hate Alek had harbored against her for changing his life forever, and without warning, when she uttered the words, "I'm pregnant." Evie couldn't blame him or herself, but that did not change the underlying resentment they each had for one another. The cruelest irony was their cycle of resentment, confession, remorse, and passion which produced three more children. It felt downright shameful. When she lay in Alek's arms she despised herself for lying with him again.

Alek's strong smell of cigarettes, sweat, and salted meats from working at the deli counter all day humbled Evie's sense of beauty and her own worth. She had married the deli boy and that was all he was ever going to be. And she was to be the deli boy's wife and that was all she would ever be. And it was coming to this understanding after their fourth child, Michael, was born, that she knew she would collapse, simply not exist, if she had to spend another minute thinking about the deli boy's supper, his insistence that he only needed to bathe once a week, or his unmerciful temper that flared whenever there was the slightest hint of disorder or disrespect.

Vinnie had taken the brunt of his father's moods. Alek always directed his anger at Vinnie when he disapproved of Evie's lackadaisical parenting style. When Vinnie was young he bore his father's temper defiantly. He never flinched. Vinnie's eyes locked unto his father's as he received each blow meant for his mother. As he got older, he withdrew, became silent, and accepted the widening distance between his mother, his father, and himself. His attempt at maintaining his dignity spurned even more contempt and violence in his father and bound them together forever in a feeling of distrust, anguish, and eventually, hate.

Evie parked the Valiant in front of St. Anthony's School. Sister Margaret was putting on her crossing guard vest. Why had she let her parents convince her to send Vinnie and Susan to the Catholics? She could hardly afford it, and although she did agree with her mother that she was not capable of guiding her children into a spiritual life, it seemed like a lofty goal. Certainly her mother, Doris, hadn't done such a good job either. Girls like Evie, the nuns had told her, had two options, the typing pool or marriage. The realization that marriage was linked to her survival came with a fateful introduction to Alek.

She had met Alek walking home from school with her older sister Beth. It was a wintery afternoon, the sidewalks were covered in black ice. Beth had hooked her arm through Evie's to steady themselves. Beth had been telling her about a note that she passed in math class, a filthy little note, about her rival undressing in front of her bedroom window so the neighbor boys could watch. The note had been intercepted by the rival's friend. Beth had been afraid of what type of revenge possibly awaited her at school the next day. As Beth turned to show Evie her face, so she could see for herself how anxious she felt, the quick turn tripped Evie, and they both slid to the pavement, sprawled and entangled in each other's embarrassment.

Behind them Alek and his brother Zef had witnessed the fall and ran to the girls. Alek had reached for Evie, and Zef had reached for Beth. The two girls now stood with the two boys, each and in their own way recognized, then understood, the instant attraction between Evie and Alek. Evie thought Alek handsome, his olive skin, deep brown eyes, and black hair would be a problem for her parents, but she didn't care. She had hidden boyfriends they would not approve of before. Her parents were Welsh, light skinned, blue-eyed, and expected her and her sisters to stay with their own kind.

"I'm Alek," he said, as he brushed the snow from the hem of her navy blue tweed coat.

"I'm Evie. This is my sister Beth," Evie said. She looked down at the top of Alek's head, his black hair greased and combed neatly at the nape of his neck in a perfect V.

"Can we walk you home?" Zef asked, offering his arm to Beth.

Beth and Evie had linked arms with the boys. They had exchanged a lot of information about themselves in just a few blocks. The boys went to the public school and were Albanian. Evie and Beth had never heard of Albania. Zef drew a map of Europe in the snow to show them how close it was to Italy and Greece. The boys walked the girls as far as the corner near their house. Evie and Alek lingered for a moment as Beth went ahead. And it was this moment at the corner that had filled Evie with a deep and persistent regret.

If only she had gone ahead with Beth and not planned a secret outing with Alek. If only she had worn her gloves and not felt a rising excitement as her bare hand wrapped around Alek's bicep or when their shoulders touched as they walked slowly across the treacherous pavement. In that moment that Evie and Alek stood on the corner, his brown eyes grazed over her face, curious, so different from how other boys had looked at her. He had looked at her with bemusement and what she thought was a kind of love, something was so familiar about him even though he was from a place she had never heard of. They had planned to meet after school the next day.

And Evie's other deepest regret was that she never told Beth, who had waited on the front steps to hear every detail, about what Evie and Alek had talked about. Beth was always sensible and helpful to Evie. She had tried her hardest to help Evie not lie or be deceitful to her friends and parents, which had been her habit since she could talk. Evie had been scolded for lying so many times, often harshly by their father, but that never deterred her. Beth feared for Evie more than Evie feared for herself. If Evie had told Beth about her secret meeting with Alek, Beth would have threatened to tell her parents, or perhaps even just gone with Evie as a kind of chaperone. And if Beth had gone with her, Evie would not have been so easily convinced to take the long way home through the park. And Beth would have forbid Evie to squeeze through the gate at the park house with Alek. And Beth would have absolutely stopped her from kissing Alek and letting him unbutton her coat, then her dress, and so on until they had gone so far with their actions that a City Hall wedding would be planned four months later and a son would be born five months from then, Vincent Michael Korli, her Vinnie.

Evie's kitten heels clacked across the tiled hall as she checked room numbers. Sister Mary had told her Vinnie was with the new priest who was starting a Youth Program. She would find Vinnie there. At the end of the hall Evie realized she had to go to the third floor and ran up the stairs, since she had only ten minutes to get back to Dell's. Evie pushed opened the stairwell door right into Howard.

"Are you okay?" Howard asked, adjusting his glasses.

"Oh my goodness, So sorry Father. I got called at work. I've only a few minutes to pick up my son. Vinnie."

"You're Vinnie's mother?"

"Yes. I'm sorry he's in trouble again. He was trouble right from the start. He got kicked out of kindergarten for smash'n a kid in the head with a block. First day, they called me to come get him. I'm always running to pick him up."

"Well, he's right in here," Howard said, pointing towards his office.

"Oh! You must be the new priest — Father Russo right?" Evie said, tucking her hair behind her ear as Howard stared at her, captivated by her nervousness.

"Yes. I'm Father Howard Russo. Come in. Here, have a seat next to Vinnie," Howard said as he gestured at the chair next to Vinnie, who had quite obviously been in a fight. His clothes were disheveled. His hair was wet and he had a blooming swollen lip.

"Oh Vinnie. What happened?"

"Nothing."

"You're a mess. Tell me. Now!"

"Vinnie had a fight in the boys' bathroom. He put one of his classmates head in the toilet and flushed it. The boy's friends, in retaliation, did the same to Vinnie," Howard said and folded his hands solemnly so as not to laugh.

"Is this true? Vinnie?"

Vinnie shrugged. He was never quite sure if his mother wanted him to tell the truth or not. He knew she wanted him to be good, and he liked when she looked deep in his eyes when she asked him a serious question.

"Not exactly."

"Get your coat. Go to the car!" Evie said.

She undid the top button of her own coat. Her chair was in front of the window and the sun poured in directly onto her face like a spotlight. Vinnie sulked as he left the room.

"Your boy needs prayers and guidance," Howard said, and wondered whether Evie knew she had a dark hair protruding from her jaw line.

"No Father Russo. He needs a dad. His father left us last year. It's been tough. Though his father was a total jer... I mean not really the best role model. He was hard on Vinnie."

Evie shifted in her seat, unsure of why she had just lied to a priest. Alek had not left the family; she had left Alek. This wasn't the first time she had relayed this version of the dissolution of her marriage. People were more accepting of her new status when they thought she was abandoned by her husband, and the tiny shrug she gave when they often asked if there was another woman, did not suggest no, nor did it suggest yes, which then encouraged people's sympathy and attempts at consolation.

"How many children are there?"

"Four. Vinnie's the oldest. But I have to say, he's good with the other kids. School's just not for him."

"Well Mrs.?"

"Mrs. Evelyn Korli, but everyone just calls me Evie."

"Well Mrs. Evie Korli. I'd have liked to have met you under better circumstances. I'll call Vinnie in for counseling and prayer during the week. Maybe that'll help."

"Thank you. Thank you Father. I 'preciate your interest in helping my boy."

"We're starting a boys' basketball team, do you think Vinnie might like to join?"

"Sure, I guess. Will he have to stay after school? He helps with the kids you know."

"Well, let me work on that, maybe we can schedule practice during lunch hour. I'm sure there are other boys who have responsibilities at home as well," Howard said as Evie stood and knocked her purse to the floor. The contents laid at Howard's feet; food stamps, cigarettes, lighters, dinner mints, lipstick, change purse, a photo of Vinnie, Susan, JoBeth and Michael, and a pair of stockings. Howard watched as Evie gathered the things from the floor and put them in her purse. He stooped to help her and found himself holding Evie's stockings. She snatched them from him and stuffed them in her coat pocket. Howard's neck reddened and splotched as he turned to open the door. Evie stood and straightened herself again.

"So sorry," Howard said, looking down at his shoes. He had missed a spot near the arch, it was quite scuffed and noticeable. He wondered if Evie noticed as well. There was an awkward silence until Evie apologized too, "Oh no, I'm sorry, it's just been one of those days. I gotta go, so sorry," Evie voice trembled a little. She clutched her purse to her chest as she fled the office. Howard stared after her. Frozen. He was aware of a familiar feeling bubbling up, a hidden desire, and 'it kept him on tenterhooks,' as his father liked to say whenever he relayed the final minutes of a boxing match he had attended.

Evie reminded Howard of a neighbor girl he had grown fond of when he was a young boy. He must have been eight or so. Her name was Margot. He liked to watch her practice cursive. With a strong command of the loops and bends, her lean fingers pressed against the pencil, she made row after row of a perfect a, then an e then i's and so on. Her delicate wrist angled perfectly across the paper, bent to a rhythm deep within, a concerted effort to bring grace and perfection to the lines before her. Evie's hands were similar to Margot's, with few lines, the nails painted a soft translucent pink that allowed the white moons to show through. He hadn't thought of Margot for a very long time, or given notice to the kind of feelings that stirred deep enough to interrupt his breath. He exhaled loudly and in doing so regained the present and marched over to his desk, opened the top drawer, and withdrew his bible. The cold leather, the black cover, the gold embossed cross gave him comfort. He sat down and opened it to Mark. But before his eyes lay on the first word, he looked at the window once more and saw Evie and Vinnie in a dispute.

Evie leaned into the car through the passenger window. She appeared to be striking Vinnie with her purse, the very purse that had held the stockings. The very reason Howard had the bible open on his lap — the stockings, the ones he held just moments ago were lodged deep in his sensory memory and part of him now. The black laced top of the stocking had caught on his watch winder and the thinnest strand of thread hung from his wrist. He raised his watch to his mouth and pulled the thread from the winder with his teeth as he watched Vinnie roll up the window and lock all the doors. Evie started to bang on the windows, circling the car like a thief, checking to be sure each door was locked. Howard opened the window so he could hear them.

"What is wrong with you?" Evie voice shook as she threw her purse to the ground, "I can't take it anymore. You stupid —." Evie stopped herself and leaned against the door. Vinnie stared ahead ignoring her. Evie caught her breath then started in again.

"Open the door Vinnie," Evie said even more frantic.

Vinnie looked at her and made a monkey face and scratched under his arms.

"Open the goddamn door you little brat!" Evie said, alarmed by her words and hoped Sister Margaret didn't hear her.

Finally, Vinnie reached over and opened the door. Evie got in and refused to look at him. She started the car, sifted through the ashtray for a decent length butt to light and snapped off the radio. Vinnie leaned his head on the window. Howard sighed, relieved when Evie reached over and held Vinnie's hand. Her beautiful hand entwined in her son's was more than Howard could bear. He closed the window, sat down again, and returned to Mark. "For there is nothing hidden, except to be disclosed; nor is anything secret, except to come to light."

Evie and Vinnie stood on the steps of an aluminum sided flat. The screen was missing from the top panel of the door. Vinnie reached through to knock on the door. Evie dug through her purse, pulled out her wallet. Annie, a pale, flaccid woman of brothel pallor opened the door. She made a somber effort to say a simple hello. She had one child wrapped around her leg and held Michael to her breast, a cigarette was wedged between her lips. She bent slightly forward to be sure the ash didn't fall on Michael's head.

"You're here early?" Annie twisted even more as the ash readied to fall.

"Yeah, Vinnie got himself in a mess at school again. We'll just get the kids early today," Evie said.

She watched the ash fall to the ground, just missing Michael's head.

"You still gotta pay the full day, ya know," Annie said.

She pulled Michael off her breast and burped him over her shoulder.

"I know Annie, of course. It ain't your fault. I'll probably have to work the late shift too cause of missing all this time."

"Vinnie here, take Michael," Vinnie snuggled Michael close to his face. He untucked his shirttail and wiped some spit up from Michael's face.

"I'll go get JoBeth. They're all up there listening to *Puff the Magic Dragon* for the hundredth time. I hate that goddamn song," Annie grumbled and with the child still clinging to her leg, started to climb the stairs causing the child to break free and follow behind.

"I hear ya. She does the same at home," Evie said. She wished Annie hadn't ignored the child and picked her up instead. Annie looked back and saw Evie's look of concern and hoisted the little skirt-hugger onto her hip, let out a troubled sigh, and continued up the staircase.

While Annie was gone Evie watched Vinnie with Michael. He was my boy, my boy, not his father's. She felt the anguish of shame as she kissed him on his forehead near the spot where Alek's hand left his first mark. When Vinnie was just six years old, Alek had backhanded him for disobeying. Vinnie, dizzy with the pain, fell against the edge of the kitchen table. The metal rim sliced open his head. Alek had little patience for Vinnie's headstrong ways and saw each misdeed as a contest to be won. "He's six!"

Evie said as she pressed a washcloth against the wound to stop the blood. "He needs to learn sometime," Alek retorted and took his dinner plate to the living room and finished his meal in front of the television. Evie had slept in Vinnie's room the rest of the week hoping Alek would apologize to Vinnie.

What would she do without Vinnie? They stood idly and waited for Annie to return. JoBeth bound down the stairs ahead of Annie, her Snoopy sweatshirt was covered in ketchup and splattered with grape juice. Her hair was a tangled mess, except for a few wisps pinned up with tiny pink butterfly barrette.

"Mommy!" JoBeth hugged her first then wrapped her little arms around Vinnie's legs.

"Hey JoBeth, careful of Michael," Vinnie said.

He pulled Michael in closer and leaned over to kiss JoBeth on the top her head.

"What'll I do when Susan gets here after school?" Annie asked.

"Just send her home. Vinnie will be there," Evie said.

She handed her ten dollars. Annie licked her thumb and sifted through the pile of ones carefully. It was all there.

"See you tomorrow," Evie said thinly, her patience worn by Annie's indifference.

Annie nodded, closed, then latched the door.

The four of them walked to the vacant lot across the street where Evie had parked. A few feet from the sidewalk, an old smoke-colored dog poked through a trash can. Its dark gray tail tucked between its lean legs suspended any fear they may have felt. Vinnie sat with Michael in the back of the car. JoBeth sat up front with Evie. Evie turned on the radio to drown out the whine in the engine. The car went forward with the first try. Evie could see Vinnie's deep sense of contentment as he bounced Michael on his knee and sang along to *Build Me Up, Buttercup*. JoBeth rocked in her seat and hummed along too.

If all the world was as Evie wished, she would have retrieved Susan and driven off to a new life, to a new town, where she would start over. She would tell everyone she was a widow and that her husband died in an accident; a terrible accident that she would rather not speak of. She would find a rich, handsome man who could support her and her children. She would wake early to prepare breakfast and send her new husband off to his job at a bank, or maybe even a law firm. Then she would spend the rest of the morning tidying the house. Her new husband would be generous and provide her with a proper household allowance to shop for the things they needed when they needed them. She would never have to scrimp and save, or do without. In the early afternoons she would walk the children home from school and plan the evening meal. After supper she would tend to a beautiful rose garden while the children did their homework. Her children would be well-dressed, polite, and excel at school and sports. Her new husband would be patient and like her just as she was.

"Mommy, are we going home, or to your work?" JoBeth asked as she unrolled the window and swung her arm out.

"Home, sweetie. Vinnie will make dinner and Susan will help you with your bath. I'll be home in time to tuck you in."

"Aw Mommy can't I go with you?"

"No, sweetie, not today."

'But I wanna see Stan."

"Vinnie, you okay with dinner? There's some macaroni and cheese and some frozen dinners. Whichever you want," Evie said, ignoring JoBeth's whining.

"Frozen dinners!" JoBeth yelled.

"Sure, JoBeth, you'll get to choose first. Just keep quiet, Michael's starting to sleep," Vinnie said and held his finger to his lips to shush her. JoBeth held her fingers to her lips and shushed too. Evie turned down the radio. They rode in silence. Each trying their best to be quiet. Each feeling the vibration of those last shushes and the reasons for it, understanding that each depended on the other, and that they were in every way a family.

Vinnie set Michael on the seat. "When'll you be home Ma?" Vinnie asked as he tucked the blanket around Michael. He was still asleep even though he vigorously gnawed his pacifier. JoBeth hopped out of the car and waited on the top step and ground away at the crumbling cement.

"Stop it JoBeth, you'll drag that mess into the house," Vinnie his voice a bit harsher than he intended. JoBeth stopped suddenly when she realized what she was doing.

"Sorry Vinnie."

"Nothing to be sorry for JoBeth, just don't want to have to clean up another mess," Vinnie said and felt ashamed of the tone he had used. JoBeth was tenderhearted and exasperating when she felt slighted. He tried to keep an even tone with her or she would bust into tears that took a long time to subside. Susan always used a flat tone with her, never raised her voice, or added alarm, an approach that kept JoBeth pliable and complicit. When Susan was around Vinnie tended to Michael, and Susan tended to

JoBeth, and this unspoken arrangement between them allowed a sense of stability and habit to develop in their new home.

"JoBeth, come get Vinnie's books so he can do his homework later."

JoBeth ran back to the car, grabbed the books and hugged Evie once more.

"I want to come with you!" Evie kissed JoBeth's cheeks, then the tip of her nose,

"Maybe next time, I'll ask Stan for you."

JoBeth pouted as walked toward Vinnie. He bent down so she could grab the key from around his neck.

"Be sure to lock the door, but listen for Susan," Evie yelled out the window as she started the car. JoBeth unlocked the door and held it open for Vinnie. She followed Vinnie closely up the stairs. Susan usually held her hand when they ascended the unlit hallway, its mint green walls were pitted with dust and debris. Remnants of dog fur, gum wrappers, and lint littered the crevices of the stairs, and around the newel posts. The single bulb at the base of the stairwell barely lit the hall up to the tenth step, which was how high Susan let JoBeth climb before she insisted they held hands. Susan didn't want JoBeth to know she was scared too, and tried her best to make a game of entering and leaving the house. Two men lived downstairs. If they made too much noise on the steps, their door cracked open and the larger of the two men poked his head out and roared, "Keep it down out there," or "Pick up yer goddam feet ya little welfare rats." JoBeth had no idea what welfare meant but she didn't like the word rat ever since she saw her first one rummaging through the garbage on the back porch. It was so big she thought it was a cat and called for Vinnie and Susan to come see. He took one look, pushed JoBeth aside, grabbed a broom, and killed it with several blows. Susan stuck her hand inside a garbage bag and picked it up, turned the bag inside out, tied it up, and threw it out the porch window into the yard and said, "Don't worry JoBeth, it's dead."

Stan crept up beside Evie and whispered in her ear, "I said thirty minutes. It's been over an hour. What the hell Evie?"

"I had to pick up all the kids. And my crap car keeps getting stuck in reverse," Evie said as she tied on her apron, "I'll stay late."

"You can't keep doing this. Last time!" Stan said even closer to Evie's ear, not wanting to be heard by the other waitresses. Evie headed out to the dining room and started setting a table.

"Don't even think you're getting the next table," Arlene, a petite Italian waitress, said under her breath as she smiled at Stan across the room.

"Why would I? I'll wait my turn," Evie said and smiled too. Confused, Stan shrugged his shoulders, turned away, and gave his full attention to the reservation book.

"That's right princess. Just 'cause your Stan's darling doesn't mean we aren't watching you."

"I had to pick up my kids. Give me a break."

"You get all the breaks around here princess."

"I'm a Queen — The Queen of Dells," Evie said, straightening herself to appear even taller. Evie's long lean legs often provoked short women like Arlene. Despite her best efforts to fit in, Arlene and the others dismissed her attempts to converse and suddenly dispersed if Evie approached them. Evie gave up and focused on Stan. He was her only real friend right now, and maybe Max now too, he had finally smiled at her. Even though she lied right to Stan's face, he hired her on the spot. The quiet desperation she had tried to conceal had appealed to Stan instantly. "You'll do well," he said and had run his thumb over the tips of his fingers, knowing she was inexperienced and this was probably her first job. Evie had told Stan that her husband had left her, which was false, that she only had one child, which was false, and that she had waitress experience, which was false, and that she had child care, which was kind of true. Without this job, without Stan's patience, Evie would be still at her parents; the seven of them crowded in a two bedroom townhouse in West Hills.

At the sixth hour of Evie's shift, the run in her stocking had become a gaping hole. Arlene had pushed in front of her to use the employee wash room. So Evie grabbed her purse from her locker, nodded to the coat check girl, and fought her way through the racks of fake fur coats and tweedy hats to change her nylons. Balanced on one foot Evie slid her leg into the black sock, fastened it to her garter, then slipped her foot into her favorite purple kitten heels.

Her first day at Dell's she had worn her black patent leather stilettos. The other waitresses chided her, "You'll last till noon in those." After just two hours of trotting across the unpadded carpet and tiled kitchen floor, her smile waned. The hostess took pity on her and showed her how to bind her third and fourth toes together with scotch tape to relieve the pressure. It worked, but she returned the next day in her kitten heels, refusing to even consider the clunky white shoes the other waitresses suggested she buy. As she pushed the torn nylon deep into her purse, she remembered Father Russo holding the very stocking that was now on her leg, his flustered look, his watch caught on the lace.

Before she left the coat room, Evie rifled through the pockets of the coats nearest to her. She was sad to have only found a few coins, a crumpled pack of cigarettes, and some bobby pins, she shoved them into her purse anyway. At the same instant Evie emerged from the racks, the coat check girl handed a ticket to a teen in a baby blue tuxedo. Another night of prom queens sneaking into the bathroom to smoke and prom kings slinking out the side door to slug down cheap whiskey from aluminum flasks. She hurried back to the dining room, three more parties had been seated in her station. She grabbed her pad and pencil from her apron pocket, and headed to the single party first.

"Father Russo?" Evie couldn't suppress her surprise.

"Hello," Howard said, the word sounding false even though he had practiced the whole way to the restaurant. Hello he had said to himself. Hell-o. Hi. Hi! He had settled on a simple Hello as he parked car into one of the last open spaces in Dell's lot.

"Have you been here before?" Evie regretted asking. She was concerned that she should have just asked for his order.

"No. The housekeeper was off today so I thought I would come out and get a bite to eat. Do you work here?"

"Well…," Evie said and looked down at her uniform.

"Of course. That was a silly thing to ask," Howard wrestled with the oversized menu.

"What can I get you tonight?

"What's good?"

"Steaks are pretty good and the pork chops. But stay away from the seafood," Evie cupped her hand next to her mouth, "Its made people sick."

"Okay then, I'll have a steak."

"Anything to drink? A cola, ginger ale?"

"Martini, extra dry vermouth, with two olives," Howard said as he pointed to the list of drinks on the menu.

"Oh, um sure. Be right back," Evie said confused. Were priests allowed to drink? She'd ask the bartender Leo, he'd know.

"Leo, Leo," Evie said as she motioned for him to come close to her.

"What's up, beautiful?"

"Can priests drink?"

"What?"

"Priests, can they drink martinis?"

"Oh sweetness, my dear, priests drink, they drink plenty. Why do you ask?"

"Cause our new priest, Father Russo, is at my station and ordered a martini like he was asking for a milkshake."

Howard watched Evie as she whispered to the bartender, a strong looking Irishman with silty blonde hair and a wing of freckles across his square face. His thick wrists protruded from the sleeves of a black and white checked broadcloth shirt. The tip of a black string tie was tucked into his trousers, Howard guessed so it didn't get wet from when he wiped down the bar and cleaned glasses. He smiled at Evie in a smooth, at your service, kind of way. Howard's envy of the bartender prevented him from removing his gaze quickly enough and was embarrassed when Evie blinked at him in disbelief. He quickly lowered his eyes and tried to concentrate on the menu.

"Did you want something else?" Evie asked.

She placed the martini in front of Howard.

"No. Thank you. I was just looking at the desserts," Howard said, trying to keep his voice light to hide the sudden disgust he felt for himself. Why was he here? How did he let himself get into this embarrassing situation? With each passing moment he felt more conspicuous than any other time in his life.

Earlier, the housekeeper, Mrs. Fletcher, had prepared him a dinner of boiled chicken, green beans, and potatoes. A fine meal. A meal he had blessed and eaten as his dinner. Mrs. Fletcher had offered him a slice of key lime pie which he declined because his thoughts had turned to Evie and her stockings, and her thief-like motions circling the car, her purse thrown to the ground, and the curve of her backside as she bent over to pick up the contents for a second time, and her hands — her hand holding her child's hand. He was shameless in letting his mind wander, to let the impure thoughts guide the words coming from his mouth.

"Mrs. Fletcher that was a fine meal. However, I think I will go out for dessert. Is there a place nearby? Howard had asked.

"Well, let's see, there's the Woolworth counter on Central. I like their chocolate pudding pie."

"Is there a steakhouse nearby where they might have a slice of cheesecake on the menu? I think I heard of a place from one of the parishioners," Howard bold in his lie, felt a sharp dread in his chest. Mrs. Fletcher cleared the plates while Howard put the butter and bread in the refrigerator.

"Oh, you must mean Dell's. That's the closest place, it's real nice there. I'm sure they'll have something you'll like."

Howard thanked Mrs. Fletcher, lifted his keys from the hook by the door, put on his overcoat, yelled good evening so Mrs. Fletcher could hear him, had got in his car and drove to Dell's.

"Father, you haven't even had your supper yet. You must be hungry," Evie said and took the menu from Howard, turned it right side up, and handed it back to him.

"No wonder I couldn't find anything," Howard said, a slight heat crept up his neck as he carefully looked over the desserts.

"I'll bring your supper in just a minute, be right back."

Howard watched Evie disappear into the kitchen and then return to the bar when the bartender motioned for her to come back. He had another martini on a tray.

"This one's on the house," Leo said to Evie and nodded toward Howard.

Howard nodded in return and then unintentionally raised his hand to wave, caught himself, and instead adjusted his collar. His collar. He had forgotten to remove his clerical collar. How could he have been so stupid to leave it on? Howard looked around for the men's room and was dismayed to see it was in the far corner of the dining room. He inched his way out of the chair and kept his head down as he walked across the dining room. Inside the men's room, Howard removed his collar and felt immediate regret. He put the collar back on, left the men's room, strode back across the dining room to his seat, and let himself feel the wrongness of wearing his collar while he sipped his drink. He knew that all priests struggled with feelings of infatuation without abandoning their ultimate purpose to serve the Lord. He would simply seek forgiveness at confession next week. And, no one had noticed his absence anyway. He was relieved to see Evie was still at the bar talking to the bartender.

"How come on the house, you never do that?" Evie asked Leo.

"Cause I'm a good Catholic," Leo said and waved to Howard. And this time Howard waved back.

"Well, this one's on the house Father. Leo, our bartender, wants to be a good Catholic," Evie said, smiling at him.

"Don't we all," Howard said, surprised by his candidness. He felt ridiculous with the two martinis in front of him; so he finished the first one in a few gulps and handed the empty glass to Evie. He was sure this probably was something to worry about. For a moment he tried to look at himself as others might see him.

Mrs. Fletcher thought he was a young handsome priest who went out for dessert. Evie, must think him a hungry priest who had ordered a drink, a full dinner, and was anticipating dessert before he had even eaten his supper. The bartender perhaps thinks of him as priest who likes martinis and wants Howard to relieve his guilt about something he did or said recently. And that guilt provoked the making of another martini to offer free as a way to repent and appear a good Catholic. And, Howard too, felt as he looked at his own reflection in the mirrored wall, a sense of adventure. He was a priest out for dinner, alone, being waited on by a beautiful woman in a short black uniform with black stockinged legs and purple high heels, a parishioner — his parishioner.

The late hour of the night with the beauty of the cold vodka, lessened the shame Howard had felt earlier, and loosened the truth from his often solemn perception of himself. He meant to be virtuous in thought and action. He intended the very best in the world, he thought as he finished the second martini, and pushed the plate away of half eaten steak and untouched fries.

"Dessert still Father?" Evie said, her pencil poised to write down his request on her pad.

"No, I think that's enough for me this evening," Howard said. He looked out the window now, and a sense of distance between he, Howard the priest, and Howard the man, stole over him and then changed into a moment of light-heartedness, of folly, as he reached over and held Evie's forearm. Evie put her hand over his.

"Father, you feeling okay?"

"Yes, I'm feeling just fine Evie. I wanted to thank you for this wonderful evening."

"You're welcome Father, very welcome," Evie said, pulling her hand away to tuck her hair behind her ear before she leaned in to gather the plate and glass.

"I'll get the check, then?"

"Yes. Of course."

Howard paid the bill from the wallet Sister Anne had given him. In one sleeve of the plastic folio he put what was owed, in the other sleeve he put two one hundred dollar bills. He put on his overcoat and headed toward the door.

"Good night. Thank you Evie."

"Good night Father, see ya Sunday."

"Oh yes — Sunday. I'll see you Sunday," Howard said, and shook out his rumpled pant leg as he opened the door into the cool spring evening.

Evie watched him as he walked across the parking lot, the wind scooped up a pile of leaves, and a polished light from the streetlamp threw the priest's shadow onto the adjacent building. The infinite dark alit something inside her, as she watched his shadow disappear. She had a keen mysterious urge to run after him even though she had no idea what she'd say when she got near him.

Evie grabbed the folio and tucked it under her arm as she stripped the table. She carried the bundle of cloths and napkins to the bin and then waited her turn at the register to cash out. Last in line, she opened the folio, added what was due to the register tray, and then opened the pocket where she expected her tip would be. Evie's hand trembled as she swiftly tucked the bills into her apron pocket, where she folded them one-handed then stuffed the small packet into her bra.

CHAPTER SIX

The next Sunday their clothes were freshly pressed and color coordinated by Susan that morning. Each family member wore a shade of blue with a neutral layer. Susan wore a navy blue pleated skirt with a grey cotton sweater set. Even though it was from Woolworth's sale rack, and a tad big, the material responded well to the iron and she added just a bit of starch to the buttonhole lining which smoothed the bulking. Susan had pressed a blue button-down shirt for Vinnie which she paired with his grey uniform slacks and a grey argyle polyester vest he had gotten from their Aunt Beth for Christmas last year. She put JoBeth in a blue and white polka-dotted pinafore, white tights, white patent leather Mary Janes, and wrapped a grey bow around her ponytail. Michael wore Vinnie's old pale blue Christening suit with its adorable little hat, the visor rested near his button nose.

As Susan adjusted the hat on Michael's tiny head he peered up at her, his green-speckled irises flickered from deep within his brown eyes. He had their father's eyes, her daddy's eyes. How she missed her father. Alek had always looked his best, even when he went off to work to the market. He stood at the hallway mirror to button the short-sleeved shirt he wore over his sleeveless undershirt. His narrow tie would be carefully knotted and adjusted, before he slipped on his one pair of continental European style trousers with their flat fronts and no cuffs. How Susan wished her father was here and going to Mass with them. She would have laid out his trousers, a white shirt, a grey tie and his grey and blue striped cardigan with its leather buttons. It wasn't quite collegiate but not grandfatherly either. Alek had instilled in her a preference for classic styles, and unlike most preteen girls, Susan was not susceptible to fads.

The current fad was gauzy materials in bright colors, like what she imagined gypsies would wear. She detested the competing colors of the loose fitting sacks that some of the older girls in the neighborhood were wearing. She had first seen people wearing these kinds of clothes at the Tulip Festival last spring. The Queen, Catherine, a girl from the Whitehall Road neighborhood, had stepped down from the stage to walk among the tulips and was immediately surrounded by a group of rambunctious boys wearing old Army Ponchos, Indian blankets, and some even had on Bermuda shorts and sandals like they were at the beach. The girls with them had daisy garlands in their hair, and long skirts with bells on them that jangled as they swirled around, their grass-stained feet lifted lightly off the ground as they spun their hands in the air like they were clearing cobwebs. Susan thought them odd, and Evie had them all look away and distracted them by giving them pennies to throw in the fountain at the Moses statute. Susan threw her penny into the green-algae water and wished that one day she would be Tulip Queen. The gold tulip-shaped crown was so beautiful and Susan imagined it sitting atop her curly brown hair, French braided and woven with ribbons.

Susan wished that someday her family could afford to dress in clean lines that created strong silhouettes, and illusions of wealth and class. Evie, too, had taught Susan to examine the stitching of a garment. She helped her understand how clothing was made, and how a double stitched hem looked so much nicer than a single stitched one. How close the stitches were determined how clothing hung on a body. Even at Woolworth's and Lodges, if you had the patience to sift through the bulging racks you could find some decent styles that washed and dried well.

On Sunday mornings Susan dressed the younger children after their bath, prompted them to clean their ears, and floss their teeth. As she brushed JoBeth's always tangled hair she would remind Vinnie to shine his shoes and to check Michael's diaper before they left. Like Sister Mary at school, Susan lined the children up and inspected their hygiene and dress. After her approval, the children waited by the door while Evie touched up her lipstick and frantically searched for her keys. Impatient with her search, Evie would yell to Vinnie, "Check the keyhole." If the keys were there, which they usually were, Vinnie would admonish Evie as he waved the keys in her face, "Why are you always yelling at us about locking the door when you leave the keys in the lock?"

"Don't smart mouth before we go to church," Evie would say as she grabbed the keys from him and scooted everyone out the door.

She always checked the mirror one more time to be sure there wasn't lipstick on her teeth. As she looked in the mirror this particular Sunday, the morning after 'the tipping' as she had come to think of the night that Father Russo came to Dell's, she noticed the red color she had chosen had crept into the corners of her mouth, making her look a bit clownish. Vinnie called from the foyer for her to hurry. Susan chimed in that they would be late if they didn't leave this very minute.

"Be right there, just one sec, get everyone in the car," Evie said, dabbing a tissue in baby oil and wiped the red from her lips. She chose instead a frosted mauve, subtle and youthful; the color evoked a natural look. It was called Beige Indecise. The shade complimented her light blue knee-length sheath. Its double stitched armholes and hem gave it a Jackie Kennedy feel. Her nude colored heels matched her nude color stockings and lengthened her legs. The illusion of four more inches added to her height of five foot eight gave her the stature and presence of a movie star. What had she been thinking when she reached for the Royal Red stick? It was clearly provocative and appropriate for Dell's clientele, but not for church. Evie looked in the long mirror once again, she looked like she felt, elegant, and tall, and poised, yes, that was the look she wanted, poised. Approachable but aloof, well-mannered yet sympathetic. She felt that this was what Father Russo would expect of her.

During Mass, Evie shushed the children, nudged them to sing the hymns, and had to go to the back of the church twice with Michael as he fussed and fidgeted, then became enraged. He screeched so loudly that Evie hurried to the church basement to alleviate the building tension from the other parishioners, who every few seconds turned their head towards her with an inquisitive look, or a demanding look to remove the screaming child from the Church. Evie quieted Michael just in time for the closing hymn. She rushed up the stairs to her seat and got there just as Father Russo gave his flock a final blessing, walked down the aisle, turned, genuflected, and blessed himself as looked over the heads of the parishioners towards the transept. He then stationed himself by the thick wooden center door that had been opened by the altar boys who had preceded him.

Evie, Vinnie, Susan, JoBeth and Michael waited in line to leave the church. Father Russo bid farewell to each parishioner. He gently held their hands in his, smoothed the cheeks of small children in their parent's arms, and laid hands upon the shoulders of the elders, or offered an elbow to help them with the step down.

Evie watched Howard's face. She finally caught his eye. He winked at her, just like Max had done, rather instinctive, like he was an old friend.

Evie looked down at Michael, unwilling to acknowledge the thoughts that flashed across her mind. Thoughts of Father Russo as a man, not as a priest. Not as the priest who just offered her Holy Communion. His deep soothing voice repeated to each parishioner "Body of Christ," and the careful nod he gave as they responded "Amen." He looked up at the chorus when it was Evie's turn, his eyes fixated on the back of the church, then his gaze passed over her, down to the Eucharist plate, her tongue out, she had wondered if he would miss her mouth. When the wafer touched her tongue, she quickly shut her lips together and looked at him. He had already moved on to Vinnie, who had stuck his tongue out and closed his eyes. Susan reminded Vinnie to say Amen. Howard waited patiently as Vinnie opened his eyes, said Amen, then quickly closed his eyes again as he waited for the wafer.

When Vinnie had made his First Communion he complained to Evie that he didn't want to stick his tongue out. He felt embarrassed and awkward as he stood in line and waited with the other children for the procession to the altar to start. Couldn't he just take the wafer from the priest and put it in his own mouth?

"Why do I have to stick my tongue out?"

"Cause it's how you do it," Evie whispered, smoothing the cowlick behind his left ear.

"I don't want to go up there," Vinnie crossed his arms, and thrust his chin in the air like a toddler ready to stomp away.

"Don't be ridiculous, you can't leave now," Evie squeezed his elbow so he would unfold his arms. Sister Margaret came along and started placing children in line by height. Seeing Evie's impatience with Vinnie, Sister Margaret guided Vinnie to a pew and sat beside him.

"What is the problem young man?" She said, placing her hand on his shoulder.

"Nothing," Vinnie said, shrugging her hand away. Evie slid into the pew behind them.

"Sister, Vinnie doesn't want to stick his tongue out to receive the sacrament," Evie forced a smile.

"This happens quite often Vinnie. We talked about it during catechism, don't you recall?"

Vinnie shook his head no.

"Oh, perhaps you missed that class," Sister Margaret offered, and looked at Evie with a conscious tilt to her head to imply that this was Evie's fault. She continued, "A priest is the only one who can hold the Eucharist. His hands have been blessed to do so."

"Why can't my hands be blessed then?" Vinnie demanded more than asked.

"If you become a priest you can have your hands blessed, but until then you will stick out your tongue. Close your eyes if that helps."

Vinnie frowned, but accepted this answer. He was eager to get out of the three piece suit, especially the vest Susan made him wear, so he got in line. Evie thanked Sister Margaret and felt relieved that she had helped prevent what could have been a terrible scene. Evie seated herself next to Alek and Susan, her mother and father sat behind them. Vinnie marched up the aisle with the other boys, said "Amen" closed his eyes, stuck out his tongue, and received the Body of Christ.

"Good morning Korli family," Howard said as he scooped Michael from Evie's arms and asked Vinnie to introduce his brother and sisters.

"Michael is the baby, Susan is there, she goes to our school too, second grade, and that's JoBeth, she's four," Vinnie said, still holding Michael's bottle, binky, and stuffed giraffe.

"Say hello to Father Russo everyone," Evie smiled at Howard, she no longer felt anxious but instead comforted by his attention and interest in her children.

"Good morning Father Russo," Vinnie, Susan and JoBeth sang out as Howard stroked Michael's face.

"He'll be just one year this summer," Evie said.

She reached out and took Michael from Howard and handed him off to Susan. Michael's little visor had shifted and now covered his eyes. Vinnie tilted the visor up from Michael's eyes and pulled the corner of the blanket from Susan's arm, wrapped it around Michael's legs and tucked it under his chin. Howard reached out for Evie's hand and held it in his own.

"Bless you," Howard said purposeful, yet reposed. He tried to disregard any feelings of familiarity that had passed between him and Evie just a few days ago.

"Thank you Father," Evie replied and willingly accepted Howard's formalities as necessary, especially after he had winked at her. Or did he? Did he, in fact, wink at her, or had she just misinterpreted that something more was happening between them? Something not clear cut but not direct either. Something that felt burdensome yet not something to shy away from, something exciting yet dangerous. Everything that was inside of her, she wanted to give to him. This odd feeling of selflessness was new and for a moment felt viable, it gave a perplexing order to her scrambled feelings.

Maybe he had something in his eye? Or too, the sun was glaring and maybe he had just squinted to see her. She shouldn't have been staring at him so intently either. Perhaps he simply just acknowledged her attempt to understand why on earth he had given her a two hundred dollar tip. The strangeness of the act, the exhilaration she felt when she saw the crisp bills tucked into the folio, had not disturbed her as one would have thought it should until she stood right here before him. And he had blessed her with focused intent, with sincerity. He demonstrated no sign of a hidden meaning in this holy act.

Howard then scooped up JoBeth. Her white Mary Janes dangled along Howard's cassock. Evie watched Howard, he was tall and handsome, his nutmeg eyes gleamed with pleasure as he held JoBeth on his hip.

"How about letting this little beauty help me bid farewell to the rest of the parishioners?" Howard asked, but didn't wait for a reply. He had already turned to the next family in line. JoBeth felt special as she stood with Howard by the gold lit doors, the vastness of the church behind them, its glimmering dome and fancy stained-glass radiated streams of colors that felt like a promise of something good to happen. Howard wrapped his arms even tighter around JoBeth as they said good bye to all the people leaving the church. "God be with you. Come back next week."

Outside Evie was greeted by her mother and father. Doris's cotton flower dress with a hand knit ivory sweater thwarted Susan's efforts to present the family as well-to-do. And even more so when she saw the shabby, but well pressed, poplin suit her grandfather wore. A pack of Pall Mall's peeked out of the top pocket and his bent grey fedora was tucked under his arm as he wiped his forehead with a handkerchief.

The early spring sun had overheated the parishioners as they exited church. Under the pear tree Howard had planted near the street, tips of purple crocuses poked through the ground. The tree was still a sapling, and despite the spiraled metal stakes that supported its trunk, it looked fragile and ready to blow over in a strong wind. Passersby would see Howard in the early mornings sometimes making three to four trips with a ceramic pot, water spilling from the spout, as he tended to the tree. Some shook their heads in disbelief, a pear tree on Central Avenue, it will surely die from overexposure to car exhaust. Others appreciated Howard's efforts to brighten the streetscape with a tree after many of the old maples and oaks were cut down when they widened the road for parking.

Evie turned back to look at Howard and JoBeth as they shook the parishioners' hands and bid them good day. JoBeth's sweet polka-dotted pinafore matched the dark blue embroidered edging of Father Russo's surplice. JoBeth looked the happiest Evie had seen her in months, her little hands reached out to each person in line, her smile big and bright, the little gap between her teeth, no longer a shadow but lit and gleaming in the violet light reflecting off the tempered glass. Evie felt tender towards her innocence, of JoBeth's apparent need to receive special attention and care from a man, from a father. JoBeth looked quite flattered and Evie, for a moment thought, rather vainly for sure, I have produced such beautiful children, and for just an instant that seemed to be what perhaps her purpose was after all. Alek and she had produced, beautiful, lovely, well-mannered children for all the world to admire. If nothing else came of their marriage, of the futility of their love, this was enough.

"Where's JoBeth off to?" Doris and Will asked as they fussed over Michael. Susan pointed towards the church door.

"I'll go retrieve the little helper, I'm sure Father Russo has to get on with his day," Will said as he noticed the last parishioner had been bid farewell, and JoBeth was whispering something in the priest's ear. Father Russo nodded and smiled as he listened then whispered something into JoBeth's ear. JoBeth giggled and held on tighter as her grandfather held his arms out to her. Father Russo handed her over, her ponytail swung from side to side as she looked up into his eyes, "Bless you my sweet child." JoBeth reached back towards Howard and kissed him on the cheek.

"Come now JoBeth, it's time to go. Father has a lot to do on Sundays," Will scooched her up higher on his hip and drew her in closer.

"Nothing more important than this," Howard replied extending his hands out in front of him in a rather foolish grand gesture.

"Well, no more dawdling for us. Good bye 'til next Sunday," Will turned, he felt the moment awkward, and uncertain. It would be difficult to say just what he felt, but the feeling dissolved momentarily as JoBeth tipped up his hat so she could see his face.

"H-A-T. Hat," JoBeth said. She liked to spell things for her grandfather. He prompted her often enough that now she just spelled things she knew for him without encouragement.

"Y-E-S," Will replied tenderly. A peculiar feeling came upon him once again, with such force that he could not ignore it. He turned abruptly and saw Father Russo, who was on the verge of closing the church doors, startled to be caught watching him and JoBeth. A glimmer of surprise appeared in each of the men's eyes as if something had been disturbed, then each assumed a formal look that stifled any acknowledgement that each had been caught doing something they shouldn't have been. Will turned back towards his family just as abruptly. He walked with them to the sidewalk. A shudder ran from the heel of his foot to the top of his spine. He wanted to ask JoBeth what she and Father Russo had whispered to one another. What could a priest possibly have to say to a four year old girl? This feeling of indiscretion lingered in his heart as his hand moved instinctively to his top pocket and offered JoBeth a butterscotch.

The heat from the gothic stone of St. Anthony's emanated to the street and converged with the exhaust from the cars on Central Avenue. The family crossed to the shady side of the street and walked away from the church doors shut and locked until next Sunday.

They walked along the avenue to the corner of Colby Street. The forsythia had just budded in Swinburne Park, the faint yellow sprouts on the branches looked like a swarm of bees resting. There on the hill, children lay on their bellies and rolled and rolled to the bottom, then staggered back up the hill to roll down again. The rising temperature and the long walk stopped Vinnie as he lifted his vest over his head, his forehead glistened; even out of the sun it was unseasonably warm. Will, too carried his fedora, the ribbon worn and in need of a replacement looked even shabbier in the bright light. Doris had removed her sweater and tied it around her waist.

"Well, Michael really caused a scene today, I thought the Jacksons were going to personally toss us out of the church," Evie said.

"That Mary Jackson wouldn't dare try, and I wouldn't worry about what she thinks after last Sunday when her nephew flicked Holy Water at his brother when they left the church. Everyone saw," Doris said as she pulled a handkerchief from her dress sleeve and dabbed her neck.

"No gossiping after such a fine mass," Will said.

"What's gossip?" JoBeth asked.

"It's something girls do," Vinnie teased.

"Not always!" Susan said, in an adult voice.

"Is too!" Vinnie fired right back at her.

"Okay, you two. See what you started Doris."

Doris stood silent for a moment, her hand on her hip as she glared at Will. Will gave her a look that was always dear to her, a side glance accompanied by a raised eyebrow. He was a handsome man, her Welsh man, who smelled of butterscotch, tobacco, and hot wool. His well-structured face always gave her pause, but that smirk, the way he pressed his lips together and scrunched his face in a slight upward smile as his eyebrows raised then arched perfectly over his amber eyes, always abated any possibility of a real feud between them. She reached out to him and stroked the thinning hair at his temple.

"Of course, of course. I should be kinder after mass. Don't pay me any mind kids," Will laced his fingers through hers before letting her go.

Doris walked ahead with Evie. Will stayed back with the children, and resumed his role as grandfather and protector. He held Michael as Vinnie tied his shoelace. He reminded Susan to hold JoBeth's hand as they crossed the street at West Lawrence.

Once across, Susan stopped in front of the newspaper stand where her father usually bought the Sunday paper, The Thoroughbred Record. Emil, the vendor, was always happy to see Alek. They would talk about the new highway being built that would stretch from Albany to Lake George, the Adirondack Northway. It would finally give them easy access to the almost abandoned Saratoga Race Track. The eagerness in which they spoke about the new road lit up their faces as if they had been given a drug for something that had ailed them. The ordinariness of the day, the leisure of a Sunday afternoon, was now full of possibility and impending wealth with the final construction of the four lane highway to Saratoga. Susan wanted to ask Emil if her father had been by, but he looked over her head, saw Evie, then turned his back, and busied himself straightening packs of gum and penny candy.

Susan looked even further up West Lawrence to the Albany Trading Port Market where her father worked. She missed going there with Evie to shop before supper. She liked seeing her father behind the deli counter with his three cornered hat and splotched white apron, its strings wrapped around his waist and tied in the back. He would pretend to wait on her like she was a stranger.

"Whatta ya have little miss?" He would say holding his pencil high in the air with an exaggerated look of inquiry.

"One pound of baloney, please," She would request and raised her finger into the air to mimic her father's pencil.

"Now do you want the phony baloney, or the baloney baloney? He would tease.

"Just the baloney baloney!" She would laugh as he handed her a slice over the counter. Susan would giggle, then would slide under the counter to give Alek a hug. Sometimes he lifted her up so she could adjust his hat and straighten his tie.

It was during these times together that Susan felt she could forgive her father for the contempt and anger he had for Vinnie. It was as if the whole world was just her and her father and there was no distance between them, no unresolved feelings or inadequacies that surfaced when she, Evie and her father were in the same room. She was his lovely daughter, and he was her handsome, funny dad, and all the advantages that this kind of love and admiration manifested was theirs, genuinely theirs. Susan lived for these moments of assurance with her father, when their hearts were wide open for all the world to see.

Susan's longing for her father happened every night at a quarter past five when Alek had usually arrived home. Evie would serve supper, and then at six o'clock Alek sat by the window with his drawing pad, a small tea tray held his pencils. In the fading afternoon light, Alek would draw, sometimes the buildings across the street, sometimes the box elm tree in front of the small flat he and Evie had moved into after Vinnie was born. When he was done warming up, Alek would call for Susan to come and be his model. With a lamp set behind her chair, Susan would sit still for an hour or so as Alek hummed a Frank Sinatra tune. He loved the old romantic songs, and his tenor voice sounded as effortless as the best of crooners.

"Turn a bit to the left, yes, chin up," Alek prompted.

"Daddy, can I draw you next?" Susan asked, as she did her best to sit still.

"Or we could work on your designs, whichever you like."

"My designs then!" Susan gave him a smile.

Susan ran to get her sketch books. She was especially excited to show her father a new hat she had designed. She thought it might look nice on his oval shaped face.

"These are coming along," Alek said as he thumbed through Susan's latest sketches. He felt sure that her special quietness was preserved on the pages in his hands, her sheer talent demonstrated her understanding of pattern, relief, and proportion. If only he had this talent when he was her age, he would have surely profited from drawing in some way, perhaps as an architect, or portrait artist for wealthy people. He certainly wouldn't be cleaning meat slicers and bickering with customers over the price of old beef bones for their soup stock.

Alek had begun to draw when he started school in the States. He had struggled with learning the language at first because he lacked the confidence and a willingness to err in his speech. He hated to look, or sound the fool. Instead he had withdrawn to his notebooks where his dignity was never far away. He felt when he opened his mouth to try to speak English an inevitable dread, and then a deep contempt for the language itself, and then the largeness of needing to learn to speak, to express himself, diminished, and instead he drew what he was thinking.

And for some time, no one had bothered him, he had looked busy, occupied. But soon teachers had begun to call on him and his mother Anastasia, and his father George, needed him to translate at the bank, or at the market, and he was called upon more and more to speak in English. His parents thought it an abomination that he had withdrawn and would not practice even just the basic words. They had come all this way, sacrificed so much, to give him a chance in America. If he did nothing else he needed to at least learn the language of the free people. His father had admonished him, then had shamed him into learning English.

Zef had helped him as best that he could. Zef over-enunciated as Alek tried his best to pronounce the simplest of words like thank you. What were these sounds? Ank? Where did you place your tongue to make such a sound? Ank? Th? Th-an-K? Alek would rather draw than contemplate how best to place his tongue between his teeth to make a sound. When Alek finally had put his mind to learning English, he had done so with the rigor and discipline of a scholar. He had stowed his drawings and pencils in a box in the closet he shared with Zef and promised to his brother he would not draw again until he had perfected his English.

The family walked four more blocks until they came to North Lake Avenue, where Evie and the children had moved. Their small second floor flat made Will's heart sink. He had liked having Evie and the four kids stay with them, the whole house seemed larger with the sound of his grandchildren's voices, their footsteps urgent and noisy on the old floorboards of their small row house. He quite liked the homelike feel that had been reconstituted with the daily necessities of caring for a family; breakfast, lunch preparation, laundry, suppers, baths, and bedtime prayers. Doris had seemed happier too. After their youngest, Edwin, had left three years earlier, there was a barren silence in the house, and in Doris.

Why did Evie feel like she had to have her own place? And why so close to the blacks? He thought of Evie and the children waking in this flat, its hollow walls letting in the sounds from the strange men who lived beneath them, the children's mattresses cold and damp upon the shabby carpet. It had been nearly three months since she left with the children, since Evie had declared herself a burden to Doris and himself. What burden? Caring for his family was not a burden, yet there was nothing he could say or do to convince Evie otherwise. Doris, too, had pleaded with her, and went as far as, in spite of herself, to point out Evie's shortcomings as a mother which only widened the already fragile divide between them. Since they left, Will shopped every Friday afternoon after work. He filled two sacks with staples and cold items like milk and cheese, climbed the dark stairwell to Evie's apartment, and left them by the door.

Doris was less forgiving of Evie's chronic lying than Will. When Evie was caught in a whopper, Doris would reprimand her, and then cajoled, and pestered Will to further scorn her. Neither Will nor Doris had been successful at shaming Evie into a being a truth teller, and this was where the greatest difficulty lay between himself and his wife of thirty years, the ever wavering tolerance they had each acquired toward Evie's questionable veracity. Neither could bear to blame the other because the lying had begun so early. It was clearly innate.

But what kind of people make a liar? Doris had struggled with this very question many a restless night after hearing one of Evie's cockamamie stories. Doris often laid awake until it was time for Will to rise for work, and then started in. Will disliked quarrels as much as he disliked inconsiderate or harsh behavior. And he felt downright uncomfortable discussing Evie when she was right in the next room. But he knew Doris was not unjust in her inquiry and that they together needed to get to the root of the problem and hasten their efforts to help Evie with her weakness.

The falsehoods Evie told were usually of no consequence other than they were little white lies. The lies often just made her seem more desirable. It was like she was decorating her person. She rarely breached the limits of plausibility, and her tales were not a manifestation of some delusion or some broader type of insanity, which Will had feared early on. Uncle Milton once had confided in him that there had been a relative a generation back, an aunt, who had been committed to an asylum and was visited only by her mother. Will sometimes defended Evie to Doris, out of compassion, and genuine love. He insisted that her motives were not bad and that when confronted with her misrepresentations she would admit them to be untrue, even if unwilling at first. And she did apologize, rather well, and with great humility.

Doris and Will had hoped that Evie's cycle of constant lying, shaming, and apology would be resolved by motherhood. They had hoped that Evie would come to the realization that as a parent she would be at a disadvantage if she continued to deceive people and that she would learn to tell the truth as she taught her children how to behave. After Vinnie was born and there was no sign that Evie's tendencies had dissipated, they both understood that the only chance any child of Evie's would have was if they were not left in her care for spiritual and civic guidance. It was then that Doris started to save money for the children to attend Catholic school.

CHAPTER SEVEN

"Housekeeper off again tonight Father?" Evie said, not surprised at all to see Howard again. It had been a few weeks since she saw him but that very morning she had woken with such a start, Howard's voice just fading from her dream state as the alarm blared. She recalled little of the dream but the inevitability of an encounter persisted all day. And here he was, ordering his supper.

"No. Not tonight. Just really enjoyed the food," Howard said.

Evie closed her eyes for an instant, then opened them. Yes he was here, Father Russo was here and he was ordering his supper. She had dreamed of him just last night, and she was quite certain all day that she would see him, and this feeling was true and he was deliberately here, he just said so himself.

"Same thing as last time, a martini too, dry with two olives?"

"Yes. That would be fine."

"Be right out," Evie said.

She dashed into the bathroom before she placed Howard's order. She had been careful in preparing for this moment, she had teased her bangs and sprayed them extra so they would hold all day. She had pressed her apron, being sure to iron the frill so it splayed around her hips rather than crumpled. She painted her fingernails a soft lavender and her lips were glazed with Stormy Pink, a frosty fuchsia color that reminded Evie of petunias. She looked as good as she possibly could in the black and white mini uniform. She did look a bit pale though, and not just tonight but the last few weeks. She pinched and twisted her cheeks until a rouge emerged from under the skin that made her look aroused rather than healthy.

Evie hesitated at the long mirror by the door, a wave of dizziness hit her and she put a hand to her head and leaned against the wall. The feeling of vertigo passed as quickly as it had come on, and before she turned from the mirror to open the door, she unfastened the top button of her uniform.

"Leo, dry martini with two olives," Evie called out and interrupted Leo's conversation with two women who had settled in at the far end of the bar. They sat cross-legged in their maxi skirts with long slits up the side, one twirled the umbrella in her glass while the other plucked a cherry off a toothpick and popped it into her mouth as Leo made them another fruity-looking drink.

"Be right there lovely," Leo assured her.

The two women turned toward Evie, assessed her quickly, and shared an exaggerated eye roll with one another as they returned to their conversation.

"I see he's back," Leo said, handing her two martinis.

"No just one."

"On the house, make sure he knows the second one is on me."

"Good Catholic again? Is this how you do penance?"

"Yup, gotta take advantage of any opportunity to repent for my bad behavior," Leo said and nodded towards the two women. Now it was Evie's turn to roll her eyes.

"They got nothing on you though, you know that right?" Leo looked sincere.

Evie shrugged. The martinis spilled over onto the cocktail napkin.

"Thank you Leo. I mean it too, I think you and Max are my only friends here," Evie said as she replaced the soggy napkins.

"And Stan too," Leo reminded her over his shoulder as he strutted to the end of the bar to finish the ladies' drinks.

"House specials for two special gals."

"Here you go Father, the second one is on the house," Evie said.

She placed the martinis in front of Howard.

"From the good Catholic, I take it," Howard looked over towards Leo and raised his glass in appreciation and then turned back to Evie, "Are you feeling okay?"

"Funny you should ask, I was feeling a bit dizzy a moment ago, but I feel fine now."

"You look tired," Howard said carefully.

"I guess I am, yes, I'm probably just tired. It's a lot sometimes working — and the kids," Evie confessed and was surprised how easy it was to talk to Howard. He nodded to show his agreement and empathy. Evie cocked her head to one side and tucked her hair behind her ear and suddenly felt terribly sorry for herself. It was if Father had looked inside her; saw her misgivings and chronic feelings of helplessness. It had been a long time since anyone acknowledged her feelings.

A deep exhaustion overcame her in the evenings as she stripped away her uniform and wrapped her flannel robe around her thinning waistline. She had been losing weight, so much so, that she had stopped wearing a girdle. The intensity of the fatigue caused tears to come on easily too, and she had cried herself to sleep more nights than not. Not wanting to wake the children, she sobbed into her pillow to muffle the sounds of her grief.

This was her own doing, Evie had reprimanded herself. It was you that packed your things and your children's things into garbage bags and laundry sacks, led JoBeth to the car and set Michael on her lap, drove to school, picked up the Vinnie and Susan, and then drove to your parent's home. It was you that told your children that you would make a new home for them without their father and that they would understand when they got older. It was you that held Susan as she sobbed and watched as Vinnie practically crawled over to her mother's favorite chair and rest his head on the arm with a look of both relief and guilt. If he had been good, and not angered his father so often would they be able to go back home he had asked Evie.

"You're a good boy Vinnie. Nothing you've done," Evie had reassured him over and over. Susan was inconsolable until Evie had showed her the box where she had packed her drawings.

"Where is the drawing Daddy did of me?" Susan had said as she frantically emptied the contents of the box.

"It was right here," Evie said, "I took the one you had taped over your bed. Here it is. Calm down now, sweetie. It's right here. See. We'll tape it over your bed in our new house."

And it was you, Evie Edwards, who decided that you would no longer live under the same roof as your husband, that the displeasure you felt at the sight of him was no longer tolerable. It was you who left the door ajar, the rooms emptied except for the marriage bed, a few pots, the percolator, and Alek's bureau where you had placed a note and your wedding band.

She had imagined leaving Alek a thousand times. The morning she left was like any other morning. Nothing particular had happened the night before. She had gone to the Albany Trading Port Market to buy pork chops and potatoes. Alek arrived home at a quarter past five. She had supper on the table soon after. After supper, Alek sat by the window and sketched, while Evie and Susan cleared the table and washed the dishes.

Susan always moved hastily so she could join Alek. Vinnie had played with Michael before pretending to do his homework. Evie had nagged the children through their baths and bedtime, folded laundry, slipped into her nightgown, kissed Alek good night as he watched the tiny black and white television, and laid in bed until her mind finally relented to the task of sleep. A welcome relief.

The next morning she left Alek. It was a sunny day, bright with hope and possibilities. After she dressed Michael and JoBeth, she put them in the playpen and washed the breakfast dishes. When the last of the plates were dried and put away, she looked around the tiny flat, and each way she turned brought the room into a sharper focus, as if she was seeing it for the first time. The yellowed linoleum floor, the tin cupboards, the fluorescent ceiling light, the stained porcelain basin and dish drain, the sputtering ice box, the mismatched chairs, and plastic table top. They were poor. Not just poor, but poor poor. Impoverished, the five of them living in a two bedroom first floor flat. JoBeth and Michael shared a crib at the foot Vinnie's bed and Susan slept in a closet for goodness sake. She understood as the dingy white wall color flickered in the rays of the fluorescence that she, Evie Edwards, was now Evie Korli, a twenty-eight year old woman with four children and an uneducated husband, living shamefully hand to mouth. She knew very well how it had all happened and she knew that to stay another minute, in this state of claustrophobia, would impede any chance of improvement in her situation. This was her consoling thought as she packed up the house, "Whatever happens can't be any worse than this."

Howard finished his second martini, careful this time to eat enough of his supper to counter any feelings of foolhardiness. He was genuinely concerned for Evie, his comment had rendered her mute after her initial response, and her self-consciousness the rest of the evening demonstrated a vulnerability Howard had not expected to see in her. She brought him his supper, then cleared his table all with a practiced smile. Each task was preceded by a hand raised to tuck her hair behind her ear. A gesture of habit that Howard found roused and alarmed him.

What were these feelings that erupted in him at the anticipation of feeling Evie near him? Even surfacing when she whisked by him with a tray of food for another table, or her hurried strides to swipe up the folios that jutted from a table's edge. Each time Evie passed him brought a wave of pleasure, then remorse. How do people live like this Howard thought, beginning to tire himself, the last attempts at comportment felt contrived and completely transparent to anyone who might scrutinize his behavior. Which is exactly what Leo was doing. He watched Father Russo, watching Evie and saw the slow dissolution of his composure as the glasses of vodka emptied. He watched Howard's eyes become untamed and eager as Evie hustled by him, her tray high over the patron's heads, her purple kitten heels drawing attention to her firm calves and taut thighs. He saw, too, when Howard slipped not one bill but several bills into the tip side of the folio, and how he glanced around not knowing who was staring at him but feeling eyes upon his deed, one that left Leo rather curious. So much so that he asked Evie about it later.

"Hey lovely, how'd you do in tips tonight? Quite the night out there," Leo asked.

Without missing a beat or even looking up Evie replied, "Oh, the usual, a few cheapskates, but not too bad." Leo watched her as she folded the last of the napkins at her station, set her tray on its stand, and pushed in the chairs at her table. She was good, he thought, the real thing. The coolness she exuded in response to the line he had crossed was barely discernible as Evie called over her shoulder good night to him, buttoned her coat and walked out the door as if it was any other night. An ordinary night.

Evie walked to her car along the pavement streaked with car oil and remnants of last night's prom; tattered ribbons from boutonnieres and wrist corsages twisted and turned in the air like little flags. The stars scattered against the blue-black sky were faint. The air was damp, brewing with the threat of a chilly spring rain. A cool breeze against her chest reminded her to refasten the top button of her uniform, but only after she secured the four crisp green one hundred dollar bills she had folded into a small square and tucked into her bra again. Father Russo had doubled his offering, and Evie wasn't a bit surprised.

"I don't think this will be too bad," Doris said.

She stirred another pinch of salt into the pot of boiling soup.

"Oh Mom, it will be fine," Evie said, "We'll give it a taste," She dipped the cracked wooden spoon into the broth, took a sip and then gave the spoon to Michael who mimicked Evie then began to gnaw on the spoon until JoBeth, hugging a tub of wax crayons, ran into the kitchen and hid under the table. The spoon fell to the floor in the flurry of footsteps that required a quieting.

"Mom! Stop her," Vinnie yelled, as he ran after JoBeth.

"Keep it down. Don't let Grandpa hear you," Doris said.

She bent over to pick up the spoon from the floor and rinsed it off in the sink before she stirred the soup again.

"She took the crayons and Susan is crying. She just wants to finish her drawing," Vinnie whispered.

"JoBeth! You give Vinnie those crayons right now," Doris held the spoon in the air to look more serious in her demand.

"No! They won't let me color. I hate them."

JoBeth held the tub even tighter and pulled a chair in closer to block any attempts at interception. Not impressed with JoBeth's efforts to shield herself, Doris yanked JoBeth by the arm from under the table and took the crayons away. She handed them to Vinnie then slapped JoBeth on her backside.

"Not another peep. Go sit down!" Doris insisted. JoBeth let out a sniffle then looked toward Evie and started to cry.

"Stop crying. Now JoBeth. Before you wake Grandpa," Evie said.

JoBeth cried even louder, "I mean it!" Evie slapped her on the leg this time. JoBeth stopped crying. Evie picked her up and set her on a chair at the table. JoBeth relented and put her head down. Evie stroked her soft brown hair until the last sniffle emerged from her tiny body. Vinnie carried the crayons back to Susan.

Doris used this quiet moment to broach the subject of Evie's apartment and the safety of the children. Clearly Vinnie did not have the kind of control that Evie insisted he had over the younger children, when he couldn't even get JoBeth to give him a bucket of crayons.

"Evie, come back here and stay with us. We didn't mind at all. Not at all."

"We're fine Mom. I have a job and Vinnie is great with the kids."

"You keep saying this about Vinnie, but he can't even keep JoBeth quiet here. What do you think happens when you leave him for all those hours?"

"Susan helps, between the two of them, JoBeth and Michael are just fine."

"Well, that neighborhood — it's just not safe — the blacks — those men downstairs from you all — just come home, let us help with the kids."

"We're fine. Stop worrying. Vinnie is fine. Susan is fine. Really Mom, we're all just fine."

"Evie. Vinnie's just a boy, an eleven year old boy!"

"I know how old my children are. Let's change the subject! What'd you think of the new priest, Father Russo?"

"Well, between you and me and the kitchen sink, he's quite handsome. Those big brown eyes and he's so tall. Makes Carey Grant look like an old boot."

"Mom! He's a priest!"

"A priest but still a man."

"I've been dying to tell you what happened last week. I had to go to school to drop off something for Vinnie. He forgot his pencil case again. I ran into Father Russo and my purse spilled all over the ground. When he was helping me pick up everything he ended up holding my fishnets! You should've seen the look on his face."

"Oh, to be a fly on the wall. A priest holding a pair of fishnet stockings! What did he say?"

"Nothing! He was beet red though when he handed them to me and then they got caught on his watch and he had to tug them off his wrist!"

"I can only imagine!"

"He came into Dell's the other night too!"

"Why so?"

"For dinner, and did you know that priests drink!"

"Drink what?"

"Well, he drinks martinis with two olives. I asked Leo, he's the bartender, if that was normal—you know."

"Is it?"

"Leo said priests drink all the time. He's served many. He even sends over an extra martini for his penance."

"I've never heard of such a thing—martinis for penance. I'm not so sure this is a good place for you to be working."

"Oh Mom it's fine. It's not like I have a lot of choices."

"You do have a choice. Go back to Alek. All marriages are difficult, why on earth did you think yours would be any different?" Doris whispered in Evie's ear, not wanting JoBeth to overhear.

"Not having this conversation again," Evie said firmly.

"Well, all that fuss and noise and it's dinner time anyway. JoBeth call everyone for dinner," Doris said, as she pulled bowls and bread plates from the cupboard.

"Dinner, dinner," JoBeth called out timidly, still afraid to yell too loudly.

As kind as Grandpa Will was, he made it clear to the household that he did not like to be disturbed during his Sunday afternoon nap. It was the only peace and quiet he had all week. Susan followed Grandpa Will to the table. Will exclaimed like he did every Sunday, "I am hungry, I am." JoBeth straightened up and Vinnie sat next to Michael who kicked at his high chair. Vinnie lifted a bib from the side arm of the chair and tied it around Michael's neck. Evie poured the children milk and put napkins on

Susan and JoBeth's laps before sitting down herself. Doris served the soup and reminded everyone it was very hot and to blow on it first. Doris finally sat down and Will bowed his head signaling the family to put their hands in prayer position.

"Heavenly Father, we who follow Jesus give you praise. Bless this food which we share for the glory of your name," Will said, still looking downward.

"Amen," they chorused with their quietest voices as they raised their heads and looked at one another with consideration. Will remembered those same looks of kinship he had shared with his brother and mother at his father's dinner table, and his heart beat with wonder and longing.

"Vinnie, maybe next Sunday you could say the blessing. I was saying it by the time I was your age. It is a family tradition we should keep. You know, I can remember my own grandfather reciting the same words, I do. It will give you comfort when you are old like me."

"Dad you are not old — not even close," Evie said.

"I can try Grandpa," Vinnie offered.

"Maybe you could write it down for him Will, so he can practice during the week," Doris said.

"Yes, yes, I can do that. Would that help Vinnie?" Will leaned in towards Vinnie and crossed his arms on the table.

"I think so, sure," Vinnie replied.

"That's a good boy," Will said.

He reached over and mussed Vinnie's hair. Vinnie smiled and felt the warmth of love that Will offered. Vinnie watched as Will huddled over his soup, lifted the spoon carefully to his mouth, blew on the steaming soup, and then slowly slurped it. Vinnie did the same.

Will had dark circles under his eyes which were from a lack of sleep and specks of soot that had sparked out of the burning garbage. Every Sunday, Vinnie and Will dragged the metal trash cans to the center of the yard and set the contents on fire. Vinnie would unravel the hose as well, readying it, just in case "things got out of control." Just last year Will had begun to allow Vinnie to strike the match and throw it on the pile of macaroni boxes, brown wrappers, and cigarette cartons. After the last of the waste burned and the ashes were stirred and assessed for any lingering embers that may reignite, they were shoveled onto the food scraps which were then added to the compost pile behind the cement locker that held the yard tools. Will turned over the compost heap several times before Vinnie set the nozzle to a sprinkle and counted to one hundred, which is the length of time Will and he thought gave the pile a good soaking. Will swept the patio area where the trash bins were stored, while Vinnie turned off the water and coiled the hose, then they both sat on the red metal chairs by the swing set.

Will and Vinnie had assembled the swing set together a couple of days after JoBeth was born. Doris thought it would keep Susan and Vinnie busy while she tried to keep the house quiet. Evie needed her rest after giving birth to JoBeth. It had been a difficult birth, one that involved a surgery and several transfusions. But they were all home and on the mend and Doris felt deeply blessed to have another baby girl to help tend to.

Alek had stopped by to help assemble the swing set on his way to work, he saw the multitude of parts and tools spread out on the lawn. Will was methodical in his work and went about projects with a plan. Alek wanted to just put the damn thing together, "it's just a swing set, not a rocket ship," he complained after Will spent nearly an hour just reading the instructions aloud to Alek and Vinnie. Vinnie didn't mind when Will read instructions ever since they had put his bike together after Alek's failed attempt to assemble the Stingray he had received for his ninth birthday. Displeased with his father's lack of proper tools and ineptness, Vinnie called Will after Alek had gone to work an evening shift.

When Will arrived the first thing they did was disassemble the bike and lay out the parts on the living room floor. He showed Vinnie the importance of understanding the instructions and then conceptualizing how the bike would become comprised of the parts before ever picking up a tool. Within an hour or so the bike was properly constructed and Vinnie had test rode it to Swinburne Park and back.

So it was without surprise that Alek had left early. He had lost his patience with Will, the new swing set, but mostly with Vinnie's eagerness to listen to instructions as if they were a matter of life or death. Vinnie was relieved that just he and Will would struggle with determining where the set should be placed in the yard and work through the little decisions, like which U pin went through which hole in the chains that held the swings. Vinnie was impressed with Will's strength as he hoisted the first red and white striped metal pole and placed it into the three foot hole. His arms had rippled with determination, his narrow face beneath the brim of his straw hat had strained with perseverance, the pole upright, Will held it in one hand as he unclenched his jaw, released the cigarette from his mouth and waved it in the air like conductor's bow, a triumph, a symphony of concerted effort.

After the swings were hung and the slide ladder was bolted on, Will and

Vinnie tried every swing, jumped up and down on the ladder, hung from the monkey bar, and threw their full weight against the poles to check that the six legged contraption could withstand the eager play of children. Satisfied that the set was stable and safe, Will called for Susan so she could play with Vinnie. Doris and Evie came out too with JoBeth in her bassinet. Doris spread a blanket on the small thyme-filled patch of lawn, helped Evie settle down, and pulled a coverlet over the bassinet to keep the sun from JoBeth's unopened eyes. Will surprised them both by stretching out on the blanket with them while they watched Vinnie and Susan challenge each other to who could swing the highest. Will rested his head on Doris's thighs and covered his face with his hat. He seldom felt this kind of peace, this kind of gratitude for the soft loving sleep that waited for him under the watchful eye of his devoted wife. He napped gently, rising when a bee buzzed by his head and Doris had swiped at it.

"Sorry dear, but I was so afraid you'd be stung."

"Wouldn't be the first time ya know," Will said. He stood, groggy with the memory of his father's bee yard. His father would have loved Doris. She was so like his own mother, strict, pragmatic, but always with a loving kindness and the intent for betterment. And if his father was alive, they would have shared a joke or two about how much Vinnie was like his brother Thomas with that same shadow of mischief following them everywhere they went. It was times like these with Doris and the children, that he didn't miss St. David's so much, that it felt a proper distance from the home he left, to the one he had made.

CHAPTER EIGHT

The morning after his second visit to Dell's Howard lay on his right side then on his left side, then back to his right side, his head throbbing, his stomach pinched from vomiting. Thank goodness Father Murphy had needed him to say Saturday evening mass instead of Sunday mass, he was in no shape to face parishioners, and especially not Evie and her family after the way he behaved last night. He felt every bit of this hangover and admonished himself for going to Dell's after saying Saturday evening mass. A revelation came to him as he examined the broken blood vessels under his nostrils in the bathroom mirror, that the bartender Leo had it out for him and he wasn't sure why. The veiny red spindles splayed towards his cheeks announced to the world that he had drunk too much. He remembered his grandfather's bulbous nose, cracked and liver purple from years of drinking homemade wine late into the evening with neighbors who took advantage of his generosity and loneliness after his grandmother had died.

The way Leo inveigled Howard to drink up and cajoled Evie into naively participating in his deception, made Howard suspect that Leo may have seen him leave Evie's tip. And what if he had? Why can't a priest help out a parishioner in need? All that good Catholic business was distasteful, and to purposefully use a heavy hand when pouring another man liquor, without having warned Howard, was objectionable at the very least, and could be considered disreputable, if he was to judge Leo's character. A bartender had responsibilities to their patrons, just as any other tradesmen. The three martinis were definitely made with more than one shot of vodka as he was accustomed.

The best thing for him to do now was to shower, then get outside for some fresh air. Mass had been over for hours and surely the parishioners would all be home now preparing their Sunday suppers. He could scarcely believe it was nearly May as he stepped out the rectory doors onto the sidewalk. His pear tree was budding and looked like it needed a good soaking. He pushed some of the mulch around the roots and hoped he would remember to water it when he returned from his walk. Across the street he could see a new florist was opening, which would be convenient for parishioners who often had to cross town to buy flowers for weddings and funerals. A green taxi sped past him as he attempted to cross the street, it brought the pounding in his head from a noticeable discomfort to a strong piercing pain. Howard pressed his face up to the dusty glass window of the florist and peered in. The coolness of the glass eased the throbbing for just a moment until a small Spanish-looking girl appeared at the door and startled him.

"May I help you?" the girl spoke English which had relieved Howard. He spoke Italian, and Latin of course, and sometimes could communicate to Spanish speakers but it had been quite a while since he had the opportunity to converse in Italian. He was certain his Spanish would be quite terrible.

"No, just stopping over to say Hello! Father Russo, from across the street," Howard said a bit too enthusiastically as he pointed to St. Anthony's.

"Hello," the girl said, unsure of what to say or do next. Her mother had left for just a few minutes and she had become frightened to see a man peering in the window but then was relieved when she saw the man was a priest.

"When are you open? Officially that is," Howard asked quietly to put the girl at ease.

"Next week. My mother will be here soon. I'll tell her you came by. Yes?" the girl said and busied herself with untying a bundle of daisies.

"Yes. I'll stop in again when she's here. What's your name?"

"Lucia."

"Well Lucia, very nice to meet you."

Lucia nodded and gave a slight wave. Howard smiled at Lucia as he waved goodbye too. Lucia blushed and lowered her head.

Howard then walked toward Swinburne Park and hoped that the budding trees and sprouting flowers would soothe the distress he felt as he mulled over his feelings for Evie and wondered whether she had told Leo about the money he had left her. Leo was a thorn in his side, so handsome, clearly vying for Evie's affection and attention, while setting up Howard to act the fool. What to do? What to do? Howard wrangled with this rising feeling of vengeance, until he entered Swinburne Park. There ahead was a swarm of girls moving this way, then that way until two girls broke loose and fled the group. A larger girl dragged a smaller girl by the hand, slowing down for just a minute as the smaller one struggled to keep up. The two girls were running toward Howard and stopped when they saw him, the swarm stopped as well and ran the other way.

"Stop! I said stop this very second," Howard yelled.

The swarm was too far away to hear, but Susan and JoBeth, the larger and smaller girl, were breathless and sweaty, and looked relieved to see Howard.

"Susan! JoBeth! What's going on here?" Howard tried to keep his voice soothing yet stern. Clearly something had been going on. The girls shook their heads and looked at their shoes. Howard bent down beside Susan, lifted her chin until she met his eyes.

"Tell me, I promise you won't get in trouble," Howard said.

"They called our Grandma the witch lady again," JoBeth blurted out.

"JoBeth shush!" Susan said as she turned to give her a stern look.

"What's this about Susan?"

"They called my grandma witch lady 'cause she wears grandpa's clothes and I kicked the one who said it first. I didn't mean to but she made JoBeth cry!" Susan began to cry herself. Howard handed her a handkerchief which she twisted and turned instead of wiping her runny nose.

"I just wanted them to stop. My grandma ain't a witch lady."

"Of course she's not."

Howard picked JoBeth up, swung her onto his hip and then held his hand out to Susan and asked, "why does she wear your grandpa's clothes?"

"Cause he died and she misses him."

"That certainly does not make her a witch lady. I can see why that would make you mad," Howard said, "Let's see if there are any tulips over here." The girls complied and looked all over for the possibility of tulips in every corner of the park. After the girls were feeling safe and that the park was their own again, Howard felt as if he had set things right, despite his hangover.

"I'll walk you young ladies home," Howard said, as he set JoBeth down next to Susan. Susan reached out for JoBeth's hand and then Howard's and the three of them headed toward Quail Street, together, ready for anything. Howard felt atop of the world. JoBeth felt safe. Susan felt quite wooly though, her sweater was sticky and ill-fitting now after the girls had tugged it out of shape, her knee socks drooped around her shins, something had kindled a heat in her core and she suddenly wanted to run to Anastasia's home to drink weak tea while JoBeth napped on a blanket in the garden filled with eggplant, cabbage, and tomatoes. She felt strange as she held Father Russo's hand. She didn't like the awkwardness of his grip and the fast gait he kept as if they were rushing from a big danger, not a small one like some stupid girls teasing her about her grandma.

"Are we headed in the right direction girls?" Father Russo asked. Susan shook her head yes and tried to keep up with his quick pace. JoBeth sucked her thumb, which she had recently started up again, despite Susan threatening to put mustard on it because she knew JoBeth hated mustard. She also tried telling her that only babies, like Michael, sucked their thumb and that she was a big sister now and couldn't do it anymore. JoBeth would agree wholeheartedly then would sneak off in a corner to soothe herself. It got worse when their mother left them overnight by themselves. JoBeth would crawl into bed with her and rock herself back to sleep as she sucked and sucked at her thumb, so much so a callous had developed around the joint.

"Okay, then, Susan why don't you point out which house is yours," Howard insisted. Susan raised a hand then retracted it. It was the first time she had seen their home as someone might look upon it. It was a dilapidated two- story home with asphalt shingles and rusted aluminum awnings. It was a sad house; the same as their old house. Susan was still waiting for the beautiful room Evie had promised her, the room with her bed under a lacy canopy and her father's drawing not taped to the wall but instead nicely framed and properly hung. Her mother had sworn that Susan would have the room every little girl dreams of, yet, she was sleeping on a mattress on the floor with her siblings nearby, and often woke to urine-soaked sheets since JoBeth was not only sucking her thumb but wetting the bed too.

The soiled sheets made extra work for Susan but she was reluctant to say anything to JoBeth about her incontinence since it seemed to Susan to be related to the move, but she wasn't quite sure and there was no one to ask. Susan would change the sheets quickly then wrapped them in a garbage bag so they wouldn't stink up the bathroom.

On Fridays, Evie had a double shift and relied on Susan to keep up with the laundry. Susan and JoBeth were in charge of washing the clothes at the laundromat around the corner. The clothes were to be brought home to dry on racks and hangars. After the clothes were dry, Susan was in charge of ironing and JoBeth did her best to help with folding. Susan taught JoBeth how to fold washcloths, socks, and underwear; the small things she could wrap her little hands around. JoBeth was fairly eager especially when Susan made a game of it. JoBeth would have to fold all the washcloths before Susan counted to ten. JoBeth would look proudly on the small stack of six cloths, as if she had just climbed a mountain, or won a contest of some sort.

One Friday afternoon, Susan and JoBeth had loaded the dirty clothes into the cart to bring to the laundromat. Susan had told JoBeth to hold onto her skirt because they needed to cross Washington Avenue. The cart was too heavy for her to push and hold JoBeth's hand. Once across she had let JoBeth run ahead to open the door. JoBeth held open the door as Susan wrangled the cart up and over the small stoop into the mat. Just as JoBeth let go of the door, a drunk slobbery man had stepped inside and lunged at Susan. She shoved the cart at him as he tried to grab JoBeth in an odd and awful manner. Susan scooped up JoBeth and had run out of the laundromat and stood on the sidewalk. Not sure what to do next, Susan held JoBeth even tighter and told her to close her eyes and cover her ears. The man was cursing and not far behind. He got close enough this time to pull at Susan's hair. She had screamed and remembered what Vinnie told her to say if anyone ever bothered her on the street. She was to look them in the eye and tell them she would rip off their head and shit down their neck. But none of those awful words had come from her mouth, just a long and loud scream. The baker from up the street heard Susan and had poked his head out the shop door and saw the girls and the drunk man. He grabbed a broom, and swung it high in the air as he headed toward the drunk man and yelled, "Get lost you old dirtbag. Come this way again and I'll call the cops." Susan took the opportunity to run as she dragged JoBeth behind her.

When they had finally made it to the house, she sat JoBeth on the couch and told her to stay put until she returned. She needed to go back to get their clothes. When Susan had returned JoBeth was still crying as she helped Susan carry the dirty laundry into the bathroom. Susan had filled the bath tub with warm water and let JoBeth add her bubble bath. They stripped down to their underwear and tee shirts, jumped up and down on the white clothes first, then rinsed and wrung them out. Then they washed the dark clothes. When Evie had arrived home the next morning, the clothes had been hung to dry on every chair, table, and hanger. She walked through the house gathered the clothes and folded them. As she started to put them into the bureau JoBeth woke.

"Mommy?"

"Yes Sweetie. Go back to sleep."

"Mommy, there was a bad man."

"What bad man?"

"At the laundry. He...," JoBeth had begun to cry again.

Evie sat beside her and drew her in, JoBeth nestled her cheek into the crook of Evie's neck, her soft tears pooled on her mother's shoulder.

"Oh sweetie, what happened? Tell me JoBeth, what happened?"

Now Susan woke too, she sat up and moved closer to her mother and JoBeth.

"Susan, what is she saying about a bad man?"

Susan too had begun to cry. She wept every tear she had stifled since they had moved into the awful house as she relayed the terrible incident to Evie. Evie had gradually quieted her two girls, soberly relieved that they were safe and unharmed, and even more determined to change their living situation. She had no idea how to do this, she thought as she tucked the blankets around her girls, and looked at their sweet faces that had finally surrendered to a deep slumber. Evie knelt beside them and prayed to God to help her, to help her children find peace in the world. She asked for a new home, a beautiful home with a proper laundry room. Before Evie undressed for bed, she removed the bottom drawer of her bureau and retrieved the envelope she had taped to it. Inside were the six one hundred dollar bills Father Russo had given her. Over three month's pay. Evie secured the enveloped and replaced the drawer as she whispered one more prayer, "Please God, please bring Father Russo to Dell's tomorrow night."

Father Russo interrupted Susan's thoughts and asked again gently, "So ladies, which of these lovely homes is yours?" He could see that Susan was clearly shamed by the poor condition of the homes before them. If he was her, he too, would not want to admit to living in one of them. How had Evie come to live in such a wretched place, and why?

"Okay, I'm going to guess that it's that one right over there," Howard said, pointing toward the grey shingled building.

"Yes!" JoBeth shouted happy that Father Russo had guessed correctly.

Susan nodded and pulled up her knee socks, as if she was preparing to walk a long distance.

"Is your mother home?" Howard asked and hoped that Evie was not.

"She's at work," Susan replied.

"Is Vinnie home then?" Howard asked, worried that the two girls would be alone in the house.

"Yes, Michael was napping so I took JoBeth to the park," Susan replied, and started to walk toward the door as she pulled the key chain over her head, then turned and said, "Com'on JoBeth." Howard wasn't sure what to do at this point. He let go of JoBeth's hand, yet, his instinct was to not let them go into that building.

"Are you sure Vinnie is there?" Howard asked, one more time, to reassure himself that the girls were in fact going to be safe.

"Yes, for sure," Susan said. She unlocked the door and reached for JoBeth's hand. JoBeth turned and waved goodbye to Howard and was still waving as Susan shut the door. Howard dropped his hand to his side and sighed, "Good Lord," he prayed, "Please keep them safe." Howard stood for a moment on the corner and looked up at the second floor windows.

He thought he saw a curtain move to one side and a figure that was about as tall as Vinnie peered out, so he waved again, desperate to be sure that whoever had looked out felt his concern and care for them. A sudden surge of deep regret prevented him from walking away, he felt he should have insisted that he walk Susan and JoBeth to their apartment door and insure that Vinnie was in fact home. And also that they locked themselves in and remind them to not open the door for anyone.

As he gazed up at the window again, the curtain moved freely this time, and JoBeth stood in the window shyly waving her little hand at him. Instead of waving this time, he brought his hand to his forehead and saluted her like she was a soldier and she returned the gesture, an image of her that Howard would remember for the rest of his life. Whenever he thought of JoBeth, how he had loved her at that moment, he standing on the corner, and she standing in the window looking down on him, her tender gaze, her small hand bent at her little wrist, her thumb tucked into her palm, as she tapped her smooth forehead above her clear blue eyes, then thrust her hand perfectly angled into the air, innocently demonstrating her unbreakable courage, her resilience.

Howard's hangover had subsided, and he returned to the rectory at a strong pace, the streets flashed by quickly as he squinted into the billowy clouds that hovered over him, his thoughts had quieted and tempered in the vigor of his gait. He had gained a renewed sense of purpose. As he crouched under his pear tree and tilted the watering can to allow a steady stream that would seep into the mulch and soak the roots, he reflected on his recreant behavior earlier; his reluctance to see Evie in the shabbiness of her domestic life. It pained him to think about his willingness to release the two little girls, who came under his protection and ward, into an unsafe and dangerous looking building because he did not want to indulge in the lusty feelings he had for their mother.

Howard, very much felt the pang of his venial sin, but the question lingered; had he acted prudently or cowardly? On one hand he felt prudence was what prohibited him from climbing the stairs with Evie's girls to assure their safety. He chose his love for God and refrained from further entertaining his sinful thoughts about Evie. On the other hand he was exhibiting cowardice in his avoidance to understand the destructive thoughts he had harbored for Evie. The sheer number of these gratuitous and dangerous thoughts had accumulated to a level of veniality that, after confession, would certainly require a long period of penance and reconciliation to restore his spiritual serenity.

Also what concerned Howard was a lecture he had remembered from Seminary that warned against taking a minor sin lightly, especially when committed deliberately or rationalized. Since no one can avoid semi-deliberate venial sins entirely, one must seek to overcome them to avoid mortal sins. The magisterium says that a number of venial sins cannot add up to a mortal sin, however, each venial sin has the power to weaken a person's will, and the more willing a person becomes in allowing such falls, the more a person will be vulnerable towards and inevitably fall into mortal sin.

And too, he had worried his absence at confession had not gone unnoticed by the head priest, Father Murphy. Howard was often distracted by his concern about what Father Murphy thought of him. Father Murphy's motives and history were unclear and seemed purposely cryptic to Howard most of the time. It gave Father Murphy a gloomy presence which made Howard feel claustrophobic anytime they were in the sacristy together.

Yet, despite his reflection and attempt to examine his conscience, he could not ignore the fire in his belly Evie had ignited. He succumbed to its flames that both burned and warmed his insides as he stood before the budding pear tree. Its lovely Anjou leaves rustled in the light wind and brushed his cheek. Howard pushed aside any further contemplation of his sinfulness and his need to restore himself into God's good graces as he climbed the stairs to the rectory door. A state of great torment stopped him at the threshold, with one foot inside the rectory and the other out, he surrendered to the duplicity of the roles that would be required of him, as both priest and suitor. He decided that he would, and must, devise a plan to help Evie find a new home for her children. This surrender to an urge he did not understand, turned swiftly to pragmatic thoughts. Clearly there was only so many times he could dine at Dell's and leave extra money, especially under that nimrod Leo's watchful eye. And quite easily and with certainty, Howard began his campaign to help Evie and her children.

CHAPTER NINE

Each Sunday afternoon, Howard gathered the collection baskets, sorted the coins and cash, then entered the amount in the ledger. When all the donations were accounted for he bundled the cash and rolled the coins, put them in a money sack, and gave it to Mrs. Fletcher to deposit at the bank. The first time Howard set aside several hundred dollars for Evie he felt completely justified. It was just a loan so to speak. As the Sundays passed, Howard insisted to Mrs. Fletcher that he could deposit the money at the bank on Mondays and that, of course, "it wasn't any trouble at all."

In August, on Monday mornings, instead of driving to the bank first, Howard drove to the Saratoga Racetrack and used the church collection money to bet on horses. Before he entered the racetrack he always removed his collar and left it in the glove compartment. That was the summer Howard learned he was lucky, it could have been beginners luck, but still luck all the same for selecting the winning horse.

On a winning streak during those few short weeks after the track opened, Howard begun to steal even more from the collection baskets and even had brazenly wagered half of that money on one horse race. The horse was named of all things, Three Martinis, and he ran the six and half furlongs on the dirt track like he was out for a stroll. When Howard learned the jockeys name was Angel Tomas Codero, it was only natural that he felt it was an omen, a sign from the heavens, to place his bet. And indeed it was. Three Martinis delivered the windfall Howard needed to buy the house for Evie. The windfall also invigorated Howard and he continued his Monday afternoon trips, not just for the money but because he began to crave the adrenaline high of the win. The anticipation of the race kept the blood pumping through his veins with the hopeful promise of a delivery of sheer exhilaration if he won.

That summer Howard had discovered a way to make money and alleviate the dullness of the monastic expectations put upon him in his role as priest. Howard had accumulated enough money for a house, furnishings, and a new Cadillac before the track closed on a humid August day.

One Monday afternoon, Howard had almost run into Leo in the parking lot. Howard had just opened the car door but quickly closed it. Leo stood just a few feet away and examined the Thoroughbred Record. Smudges of ink dotted the center of his forehead which he rubbed as he chewed on the tip of a Lucky Strike stuck in the corner of his mouth. Howard ducked down under the dashboard and peered up every few seconds until he saw that Leo had entered the pavilion. Howard was unnerved by the intensity of anger he felt toward Leo. He felt the smugness of Leo's expression bristle across his skin as he watched him swagger towards his car. He must have had a big win. Howard prayed that his feelings wouldn't disrupt his winning streak — his good luck. Yet only God knew why he was so lucky. Remembering his blessing relieved Howard of feeling small and insignificant, or shameful; of the self-doubt that Leo provoked in him. Everything was better than he could have hoped for, better than he ever deserved; this luck, while it lasted, made him feel just a tad broken-hearted. Instead of striving for spiritual serenity, Howard felt his blood boiling in his veins, his heart racing with his immersion into the life of the common man.

Howard especially felt the wrath caused by his incongruous behavior when he was in Father Murphy's presence and in the confessional. He had put their sacred place, their St. Anthony's, to an unseemly use and committed sacrilege with his thievery of money given wholeheartedly, and with good intent, by the parishioners. His willingness for such self-examination ceased when he thought of Will, Evie's father, handing JoBeth two nickels so she could contribute to the passing collection basket.

Howard had violated their trust and the immunity offered to those who entered St. Anthony's church as having the right of sanctuary. Given the gravely profane use of ecclesiastical property, his omission of the sin during confession, and his continuance to bless the Eucharist and give communion when he himself should not even receive communion, made Howard feel as if he hadn't fully understood the consequences of his decision just months ago when he stood at the threshold of the rectory and committed to helping Evie.

This path he had chosen was beyond reparation. How silly it seemed to him now that he had rationalized his lusty thoughts of Evie, when now the guilt sat not inside his head, but deep inside his heart. What Howard had done he could not undo. He was alone now, in his silent prayers, when he could ask God for forgiveness. Howard understood, with much sadness, that he had lost the privilege of participating in the commune of prayer, the immunity of priesthood. Even the most forgiving of parishioners, Howard imagined, would not grant him redemption, if ever he was brave enough to confess his sins and ask to be forgiven. Would someone like Mrs. Fletcher be willing to absolve Howard of these unimaginable deeds and allow him to forget the past and move on? Howard tried too to imagine Father Murphy's reaction to Howard's sin, or Evie's parents, or Lucia, the little florist girl, or his father and mother. What could he say to them, how would he explain the unexplainable?

The Magisterium's prescient lecture of venial sins leading to mortal sins was no longer a harbored argument, or silent discourse, but a sodding mess to Howard. His worry now was not the rapid accumulation of venial sins but what seemed like a fateful accumulation of mortal sins, which in the Old Testament were punishable by death. Howard had become a practiced liar and thief. His heart was heavy with sin, and resolved to the fact that there was no turning back now.

As the sun slid behind the rolling hills alongside the Northway, Howard spotted a billboard that advertised a new development being built along Route 20, Colony Acres. The houses were modern, vinyl sided, with large landscaped lawns and pretty white fences separating the homes. What the heck, he thought, no harm in just looking. At the end of the Northway, Howard took a right onto Route 20 until he came to an identical sign to the billboard that pointed into the beginnings of a new neighborhood. Bulldozers and trucks lined the street with homes in various stages of completion. Howard rounded a cul de sac where all the homes were finished, there he saw one he especially liked.

Two men in hard hats stood on the lawn with clipboards. The two men were serious. One was heavy lidded, freckled, and what some would call, ruddy complexioned. He was as big as a refrigerator. Square and dull. The other was squirrelly, small, an Italian looking guy with bad teeth and choppy black hair. He breathed loudly while the other one looked like he barely breathed at all. Howard got out of the car and started to approach the two men but changed his mind, and turned back toward the car. The bigger man called out to him.

"Are you lost?"

"No, not lost," Howard replied.

"Interested?" The smaller man said pointing to the house.

"Yes, I guess so, I mean I am interested."

"Come on over we'll show you around, usually the realtor is here but he took off early."

"Oh I don't want to bother you. I can come back later."

"No bother," the bigger man said, "We were about to do the inspection, you can just tag along."

Howard followed the men through the house. They pointed out how well made the floors were, showed him the intercom system, and led him into the finished basement with cedar closets. Then they took him out to the yard; a double lot surrounded by white picket fencing. There was a swimming pool, a half court, and a small wood of red pines. When Howard saw the half court it was if God had willed him there. This was the house. This was the house he would buy for Evie. Even though he had the money, he had no idea how one went about purchasing a home.

On the way back to the parish Howard pulled into Dell's and parked under a tree at the back of the lot. Evie's car wasn't there. Just as he was about to pull away, Leo walked out the side door with an empty keg. He saw Howard and shook his head incredulously. Howard was dismayed at his now seemingly bad luck. Howard felt there was nothing else he could do but roll down the window. So he did, and tried his best not to look sheepish.

"Father, she's not here," Leo said, his virility and pure calm meant to purposefully agitate Howard.

"I'm not sure what you mean, I was about to come in and then realized I forgot my wallet."

"Oh, I thought you were looking for Evie, seems like everyone is looking for her tonight."

"Everyone?" Howard asked, trying not to blink.

"Yeah, her ex stopped by just a few minutes before you. Seems like she told everyone she had to work tonight. Alek stopped by her parents' first and was on his way to her apartment."

"Well, I'm sure there's a reasonable explanation."

"Yeah, well you never know with Evie."

"Maybe she's just running late," Howard said and hoped Leo would set the keg down and return inside.

"I'll be on my way. If Mrs. Fletcher didn't start dinner, I may be back."

"If you do, remember your wallet Father," Leo said. He tossed the keg into a pile of empties as if to dismiss Howard from further humiliation. Howard rolled up the window, his stomach was uneasy, his heart palpitated out of rhythm. Keep your enemies close popped into his mind as Leo turned and waved goodbye, the smirk on his face even brighter and without concern. As Howard drove back to the parish, he remembered exactly how the saying went, keep your friends close and your enemies closer. And that was exactly how he would start the conversation with Leo when he was ready to propose his plan to him.

CHAPTER TEN

Evie walked past a man with a basket of puppies when she entered King's Department store. The puppies made a great racket and climbed over each other as they tried to escape the basket. The man picked up the puppy that got closest to the top, snuggled it close to his face, and then placed it at the bottom of the heap. Evie felt a kinship with the puppy who had to keep starting over but never gave up. She knew she would be taking it home on her way out. It was cute with its chocolate brown head and white spotted body. Almost a Dalmatian, which JoBeth would love after having begged incessantly when they left the theater showing 101 Dalmatians "Just one puppy, please mommy, please." Evie thought the movie too sad for children and that nobody as mean as Cruella should have the good fortune to be rich too.

When Evie woke that morning the starlings sung in a tree outside her bedroom window. Instead of leaping from the bed to start breakfast and get the children ready for school, she just laid there and listened to the birds, their song lovelorn, sorrowful, as if they were sharing their burden of anticipation of the next meal, or a looming rainstorm. The birds sounded like the song in Evie that whirred and stung the spot above her diaphragm and under her breastbone as if someone was pressing their thumb down on her skin, drawing it taut. There was really never a burst of sudden pain or anguish, just a constant tinge of melancholy. She knew dawdling like this she was going to be late for work but she didn't care. Stan would accept any old excuse she gave him, he always did.

"Welcome to King's," the lift operator said dryly, almost to himself.

"Good morning, third floor please," Evie said, and instinctively turned her head to the closing door and stared straight ahead.

"Children's huh? How many?" The elevator man said, this time a bit too loud.

"Four. Two girls and two boys."

"Are you sure? You look like you're still in high school."

"Yes. I'm quite sure," Evie said, surprised by her sarcasm, then quickly said, "Thank you, thanks so much," as she stepped out of the elevator and hurried toward the toy aisle. Evie loaded up her shopping bag with toys then off to the doll section, then to the musical instruments. Evie filled the checkout counter with Rock'm Sock'm Robots, paper dolls, a child's guitar, a stuffed bear, wrapping paper, and ribbon.

"Christmas shopping a bit early eh?" said the clerk.

"I guess you could say that," Evie said. She opened her wallet and used fifty of the eight hundred dollars of Father Russo's tips. She had stopped at the bank first to break one of the hundred dollar bills into smaller bills.

"Lucky kids."

"They're good kids. Just a bit of a windfall. Thought I'd treat them," Evie said, "And I may get one of those pups out there too."

Evie gathered her packages. Across from the elevator was Champ, the stupid mechanical horse that had left one of two large scars on JoBeth's face. The scars on JoBeth's face each told a story about Evie. The first scar was a half-inch long between JoBeth's eyebrows. A few months past, Evie had run into King's Department Store to get diapers for Michael. She had specifically told JoBeth that they had no money and were only getting diapers. But JoBeth insisted on riding Champ even after she said no and had snuck away. By the entrance, she stood in front of Champ by the red metal box with his name printed in gold letters, "Ride the Champ. 10 cents." A man in painter's coveralls picked JoBeth up and put her on Champ. Evie hurried toward them, but was too late. The man had walked away just as Champ lurched forward, and JoBeth flew off the saddle. Her little head slammed down on the metal base. An ambulance was called. Evie lifted JoBeth into her arms and laid her on the cot. The ambulance drivers took JoBeth away as Evie scrambled to the Valiant and followed the ambulance to the hospital, the whole time she prayed, "Please God don't let her die, take me instead." There had been so much blood.

At the emergency room, the doctor sewed up JoBeth's face, sent her home with an icepack, a Popsicle, and instructions for Evie to bring JoBeth back to have the stitches removed. When Alek and her parents saw JoBeth's face they immediately looked accusingly at Evie. "What happened?" they asked over and over again. Alek wouldn't even let Evie answer, "Don't bother with one of your stories, I'll ask JoBeth myself." And JoBeth did tell the story correctly, and for once Evie was believed and given sympathy.

The second scar was a quarter inch on the right side of JoBeth's lip which circles the inside of her cheek. Thirty stitches in all. This scar was Annie's, the babysitter's fault. When Evie arrived at the hospital, Annie was slightly drunk and slurred her words as she described what happened.

"A four year old shouldn't have such ideas," Annie started in, "she stole a bike."

"Annie, where were you? Why weren't you watching her?"

"I put her down for a nap, and the next thing I know the kids across the street are yelling that she stole the bike. So I go out and there she is flying down Colby Hill."

"JoBeth wouldn't steal a bike!"

"Well she did. And she didn't know how to stop it either. I just told her yesterday that she was too small to ride the bike and had to wait 'til next year."

The bike was a 1968 Schwinn Stingray, red with white rims and plastic-covered spokes. When Evie saw it the next day, mangled and twisted it still looked like it had been the perfect bike. Her JoBeth had snuck out of the second floor apartment, had run to the neighbor's house where the bike was parked in an alleyway, pushed it into the street, hopped on, and took off. JoBeth had told her that it was hard to pedal and even harder to stop once she reached the hill. Annie described how when she got out to the road, JoBeth had looked fearless as she stood on the pedals, her pony tail flying in the wind, as she headed down Colby Hill. The bike had moved faster than JoBeth could control, so she had pedaled even faster. Annie had shouted instructions on how to stop.

"Stop pedaling," Annie yelled, "push back on the pedals. God dammit!" JoBeth said she had heard nothing, but saw the stairs in front of her, and the aluminum screen door. JoBeth told her that Annie had stepped aside. JoBeth had hurled up and over the curb, onto the stairwell, and crashed through the screen door.

"Why didn't Annie catch me Mommy?" JoBeth bawled after she had endured the Novocain and stitching.

Evie often examined the scars. She was appalled by them. The marks on her daughter's face told the world, your mother wasn't watching you, she wasn't there to protect you.

As it happened, Leo had strutted across the parking lot as Evie stood in front of the basket of pups. He gave a big wave.

"What are you doing here?" Leo said, "You got to be at work in an hour!"

"Oh so now you're keeping track of my schedule," Evie said, with a sweetness that assured Leo she was joking.

"Pups huh? They can be a lot of work," Leo said.

"I thought it would make JoBeth happy," Evie said and pointed to the sweet brown-head male pup, "I'll take this one." Leo let out a low whistle, "Look at the size of his paws. He's going to be big," Leo said, softening as he petted the top of the pups head.

"You sure. How about this one too? The man held up a second pup, the inverse of the first pup's brown body with a white head, "Two males, the rest are girls."

"Brothers," Evie said as she put her packages down to hold the second pup. The pups wrestled for a moment then settled in, "Oh what the hell."

"Brothers it is," Leo said. He helped Evie with her packages.

"Cool. What'll you name them?" asked the man.

"Elvis and Cash. My daughter's favorites."

"JoBeth is going to one happy little girl," Leo said.

"I sure hope so."

Leo walked with Evie to her car.

"What's with all the bags?" Leo said. He peeked inside the bag that held the paper dolls and stuffed animal.

"Just a bit of shopping for the kids. They're having a hard time with their father leaving and all."

"I can imagine. You must be doing fantastic in tips to have enough for all this," Leo prodded.

"Good enough. Why are you always asking me about my tips? Are the other girls talkin'?"

Evie knew that Leo was suspicious of Howard and may have seen him leave the money in her folio the other night, but she wasn't sure and she wasn't about to confide in him. She knew he liked her too much and she didn't want to lead him on.

"No they ain't talking about you. Just looks like you're doing well, especially since Father Russo has been around. He must be bringing you some good luck." Leo was shameless now. He thought for sure Evie would have confided in him, he thought of her as his friend. And he felt that she was aware of his deepening feelings for her, and shouldn't begrudge him for asking. He had spent a few sleepless nights creating elaborate scenarios of his and Evie's future. However, taking on four mouths to feed, that were not of his own making, dampened his enthusiasm to pursue a real relationship with Evie, but he was holding out for a one-nighter if ever the opportunity presented itself.

"Father Russo was your good luck not mine, all that penance you do making him martinis is certainly adding up," Evie said, with a certainty in her voice to indicate to Leo the conversation was over.

"Well that may be true, but he was coming in to see you, not me."

"I think he's just lonely like the rest of us. But he hasn't been around for a while so why are we even talking about this?" Evie surprised herself with this candidness.

"Yeah, could be," Leo said, but shook his head no, contradicting his words.

"Well I gotta get home with all this and get ready for work. See you later."

"See you sweetness," Leo said. He opened his car door and got in.

Evie stopped, "Hey weren't you here to shop?"

"Nah, I just pulled in to see you," Leo grinned at her then drove off.

Evie noticed how much more agile and aggressive Elvis was when she put him on the floor of the back seat next to Cash who was a bit stolid and content to just sit there with his front paws under his chin. Elvis had hopped onto the front seat beside her in no time at all. Evie accepted Elvis's need to be near her and also found some comfort in his determination to sit beside her. "Hang on, little brown head," Evie said. She jammed the reverse button into its socket, "maybe you'll be the one to bring us some luck." And Elvis was just that, luck; the car backed up on the first try. Evie reached over and rolled down the passenger window, and like JoBeth, Elvis climbed onto the armrest and stuck his head out. JoBeth will love Elvis, Evie thought as she made her way home to drop off the presents and pups before she picked up the children.

At home, Evie piled the presents in the middle of the living room floor. She sat on the rug and listened to her breath just as she listened to the starlings that morning. Her breath was shallow and excited. She wanted so much to give her children the things they asked for. And now she could provide her children the things Alek would never let her buy. She wouldn't have even dared ask to get JoBeth a puppy. "Another mouth to feed? Really Evie, you're spoiled," would have most likely been Alek's reply. When she was young, and in love, she would have accepted this kind of response and probably felt stupid to ask such a silly thing of her husband. As her children got older, and wanted more, needed more, she did want a better life for them. She wanted them to feel that they could ask for the things that would help them grow into the people they needed to become, and not settle to be a shadow of their imagined selves.

As the pups tussled and romped around the kitchen, Evie felt a genuine happiness. The whirring in her midriff had subsided and it was noticeable. The very thought of the look on JoBeth's face when she held the pups brought Evie's breath to a meditative slowness, so much so that she leaned back and gently closed her eyes and rested. A complacency and ease filled her lungs and then released into a calm surrender to the peace and quiet. She was in charge of her life, her finances, and her children. Even if she wasn't the best at it, she felt damn good not having to get permission from a man, or her parents, to purchase something.

The pups finally settled down and laid by her feet as she put on her final coat of mascara. Her pressed uniform still hung loosely on her body. Evie knelt on the floor beside the pups, stroking each of them under the chin. How she wished Father Russo would come back to Dell's. Evie touched her breast bone, then her lips, then crossed her forearms as the pups nestled around her legs. She missed the money but she also missed him. She crossed herself, then folded her hands, "Oh God, please let it be your will for me to see Father Russo again. I need his help in caring for my children." There was nothing else clearer to her than those words. Howard's image came easily to her mind, his lean angular body, his olive skin, his brown eyes with deep lines at the corners, his black tousled hair, and his genuine modesty felt like a promise that at some point he would reveal more of himself. "Goodness," Evie said aloud, "I should not be having these thoughts." She rose from her knees, glanced at the pups, turned off the light and shut the door. She could hear the pups scratching to get out as she left the apartment to pick up the children.

Around the same time Evie shopped at King's, Howard had retrieved Vinnie from class for counseling. He was heartened to see that the nuns still made children stand and greet a newcomer.

"Good morning Father Russo," the children sang out as Howard entered the classroom.

"Good morning Sister Mary and good morning children. Please everyone be seated," Howard said as the children all sat at the same time.

"Sister, may I speak with you?" Howard asked.

Sister Mary nodded then walked across the room and turned off the lights. In unison the children put their heads down on the desk as Sister Mary and Howard stood outside the door of the dark classroom.

"I spoke with Mrs. Korli last week about Vinnie," Howard said, trying not to clear his throat, "I told her I would counsel and pray with Vinnie during the school day."

"Yes Father," Sister Mary said, looking pleased.

"Please ask Vinnie to come to my office after class."

"Yes, Father. This is very kind of you to take an interest in Vinnie. He is in need of some guidance."

"Thank you Sister. Just doing the work the Lord has asked of me," Howard said over his shoulder as Sister Mary opened the classroom door and turned on the lights. The children's heads rose, eager to get back to the story Sister had been reading aloud. It was a class favorite, *Black Beauty*. Sister Mary picked up the book, leaned back on the desk and continued, "We shall all have to be judged according to our works, whether they be towards man or towards beast..." When the chapter ended, Sister dismissed the class, "Everyone may go — except for Vinnie."

"Yes Sister Mary?" Vinnie asked. He stood by the door while Sister straightened her desk top. He had no idea what he had done now. He reviewed his behavior during the story, he had listened and not fidgeted. He stood when Father Russo came in and greeted him with the class. He had put his head down right away when the lights went dark. His shoes were shined, his tie was straight, he looked at his hands, his fingernails were dirty, but only because he hadn't time to wash them after recess. He had been avoiding the boy's room because the last time he went in there he ended up Father Russo's office. It wasn't that he sought out trouble, it just seemed to find him.

"Father Russo has asked that you go to his office after class," Sister replied.

"Did I do something wrong Sister?" Vinnie asked.

"No Mr. Korli, your behavior has been quite commendable today. Father wants to help you stay that way."

"Yes Sister."

"Well get along now, you know where his office is," Sister said, with a hint of amusement in her voice.

"Yes Sister," Vinnie said, with a light smile. He liked Sister Mary. She had a kind voice and often brought her guitar to school and taught the class to sing folk songs. Vinnie loved to sing *This Land is Your Land*, and he also liked *Michael Row Your Boat Ashore*, so much so that he had asked that his new brother be named Michael, and felt a mild astonishment when he peered into the hospital nursery and saw Michael Vincent Korli written on the name card. His mother had given his brother his favorite name, and his own name too. Michael pressed his head against the nursery glass what seemed like hours. A nurse saw Vinnie waiting and had pushed his brother's cradle closer. Michael finally turned his head towards the window. Vinnie could see his eyelids were red and swollen, like he had already cried up a storm. He hoped Michael would be more like him, and not like JoBeth, who cried readily and often. It wasn't that Vinnie didn't like JoBeth, or Susan for that matter, but he felt a special connection to Michael, a boy, a brother. Vinnie touched the glass, his heart beat joyously, and promised Michael to be the best big brother anyone ever had.

Vinnie ran his hands along the lockers as he headed to Father Russo's office. He took the stairs two at a time to the third floor, before opening the door he peered through the window into the hallway. He saw Father Russo exit the teachers' lounge carrying two sodas. It turned out that one would be for him. After he sat down in the chair by Father Russo's desk. Father Russo said they would talk for a little bit while they drank their sodas, then they would pray together. Vinnie thought this counseling thing didn't seem as bad as it had sounded at first. It didn't feel like a punishment to be excused from math class, drink soda at school, talk about how he behaved, and why he made the choices he made. Vinnie was accustomed to spending a whole day in the corner when he misbehaved.

Often, Father Howard asked him about his family too. Vinnie spoke freely about his mother and siblings but he was reluctant to discuss his father. He felt a sense of disloyalty and fear when the subject was broached by Father Howard; as if his very survival depended on his silence. This allegiance to his father was something that confused Vinnie, yet it was one of the strongest feelings he had — he felt it strongly and without question — it was wrong to speak ill of your father. Grandpa Will had told him many a time, "Speak well of your family, of your enemy, say nothing." Vinnie thought of his father as both his father, and his enemy. Father Russo never pushed Vinnie to answer, he would move onto a new subject and encourage Vinnie to keep talking. He leaned in and nodded his head vigorously if Vinnie described a feeling or thought he had about how he could improve his behavior. When Father Russo opened the bible and asked Vinnie to read, he didn't mind at all.

When Vinnie finished reading, Howard put his hand on Vinnie's shoulder and said, "When you say your bedtime prayers tonight I want you to ask God to help you be good. Ask him with all you heart."

"Okay Father."

"Be sure to ask God every night. He will help you."

"Is that what you do?"

Howard ignored Vinnie, "I'll see you on Friday after class. You are excused."

"Yes, Father."

Vinnie took the same route back to the classrooms, running his hands along the lockers, the ping of metal echoed behind him. Vinnie slid down the banister, then headed to the choir room to pick up Susan. Susan was front and center, her hymn book held high, her voice rose above the other girls. Vinnie tried his best to distract Susan with funny faces and then a silly walk but she would have none of it and focused straight ahead. The teacher called on Susan to solo and her posture shifted ever so slightly to open the full timbre of her voice. When she finished the solo, she held the book up even higher to block Vinnie from her line of sight. Dismissed, Susan packed up her books and lunch box and grabbed her sweater from a hook.

"Really funny, Vinnie," Susan said as she swung her lunch box at Vinnie.

"You sounded good — good as monkey butt," Vinnie teased, shoving Susan playfully. Once outside the school doors, Vinnie wrestled Susan into a half-nelson and gave her a noogie on her head. Susan's books and lunch box scattered as she laughed and begged Vinnie to stop. Howard watched them from his office window. His eyes darted between Vinnie's and Susan's face looking for clues of Evie in their expressions. Vinnie's eyes looked more like his mother's with that glint of mischief layered over their warm pools of blue-green irises. Vinnie had Evie's pale skin, chestnut hair, and thick lashes. Susan's had her father's olive skin and dark curls that she swept away from her face with bobby pins strategically crisscrossed near her ears and forehead. Howard opened the window wider to hear them.

"Vinnie, okay, okay, Uncle! I said UNCLE!" Susan said, in a still teasing voice.

"Did you say Aunt. I hear AUNT!" Vinnie said. He stuck out his tongue and slobbered the side of Susan's cheek.

"Aunt then!" Susan cried out as she squirmed and laughed.

"No it's Uncle, Butt breath!" Vinnie noogied her one last time, slobbered the other side of her cheek, then let her go.

Susan fell to the ground holding her belly still laughing. Vinnie gathered up her books, her lunch box, and sweater. He held his hand out until Susan stopped laughing and let him pull her to her feet.

"Uh-oh Vinnie, don't look up but I think Father Russo is watching. Ready to run!"

"Sure thing!" Vinnie whispered. They tore off towards home.

Howard closed the window and let out a long, tired, angry breath. He struggled the rest of the day to rid himself of the envy he felt watching Vinnie and Susan. The playfulness and sheer joy they exhibited in their silliness nursed a small stream of self-pity that Howard did not have the strength to examine.

As Evie pulled into the school parking lot she saw Vinnie and Susan running towards her. She parked and leapt from the car.

"There's Mom!" Susan yelled out.

"Mom! Mom! Over here!"

Vinnie and Susan ran toward Evie. JoBeth had crawled out the window and was running toward them now too.

"JoBeth get back here this minute," Evie yelled. JoBeth stopped and waited until Vinnie and Susan passed her then she tagged along as if she had been running with them whole time.

"Why are you running so fast?" Evie asked.

"Just racing," Vinnie said.

"I would have won too, if it wasn't for JoBeth!" Susan said. She scooped up JoBeth and hugged her.

"Aw, sorry Susan. Don't be mad."

"Not mad. How come you're not at the sitter's?"

"I picked up JoBeth and Michael 'cuz I have a surprise. And don't even think you will get me to tell you what it is!"

"I tried and she won't tell," JoBeth pouted.

"Come on, get in so we can get home!"

Susan sat up front with JoBeth and Vinnie sat in back with Michael. Evie drove slowly, teasing them until they begged her to drive faster.

"Ok. On the count of three I want you..." Vinnie had already opened the door before Evie could finish. JoBeth ran in and stopped at the pile of presents. She cocked her head, looked at Evie, then Susan, then Vinnie, then back to Evie.

"Mommy, is that a puppy?" JoBeth whispered.

"A puppy? Could be?" Evie said.

She led JoBeth to the bathroom door. Both puppies scratched at the door, eager to get out. Evie gently opened the door and Elvis and Cash busted out into the living room and promptly peed on the floor.

"I'll get some towels," Susan said as JoBeth knelt and hugged each of them.

"Uh-oh. Not supposed to do that," JoBeth said to Elvis and Cash as she stroked their heads and then tried to kiss them.

"Meet Elvis and Cash," Evie said as she knelt beside JoBeth. Susan handed her a towel to wipe up the pee.

"Cash! Oh mommy I love him."

"Johnny Cash. Your favorite," Susan said. She poked through her school bag, pulled out a pair of scissors, and began to cut out a dress for one of the paper dolls. Vinnie played Rock'm Sock'm Robots against an invisible foe. Evie sat on the floor with JoBeth and the pups.

"Okay, I got night shift tonight. Vinnie — dinner, baths, bed by eight o' clock. Be sure Michael drinks his whole bottle. Put a bit of cereal in the bottle if he fusses."

"Sure thing," Vinnie said as the blue robot knocked out the red robot.

"You can play later. I'll even play with you when I get home if you're still awake. Okay? And make some soup. Susan can help you with the grilled cheese."

"Ah, ma, can't you stay. Pleeeease," JoBeth held Cash up to her face as if he was asking Evie to stay. Evie stood, put her apron on, kissed Vinnie on both his cheeks, squeezed him tight, and picked up her purse.

"I'm really late for work now. Vinnie, I may have to stay even later than usual to make up the time. Don't open the door. For anyone!" Evie said as checked her lipstick in the hall mirror. She peeked in one more time, blew a kiss, then closed and locked the door. She jiggled the handle and yelled through the door one last time, "Remember, keep it locked, and don't open it for anyone."

"I know. I know," Vinnie said then listened as his mother finally descended the stairs, the sounds of her quick hurried steps did not provoke the men downstairs. Good, they must not be home, Vinnie thought as he tucked the stuffed bear under Michael's arm before starting another match of Rock'm Sock'm Robots. Susan focused as she carefully cut each dress, taking special care to preserve the notches so that the dress would hang properly on the doll. JoBeth dragged each puppy to her bed and fell asleep with her little guitar strapped to her.

"Hey, Susan, come play a round with me. Bet you I can beat you with one hand tied behind my back."

"In a minute, I just want to try this blouse with this skirt," Susan said, flustered by the small tabs that caused the blouse to keep slipping from the paper doll body.

"I give up," Susan sighed. She put the paper dolls in their box, and returned the scissors to her school bag.

Michael whimpered the way he did when he was about to wake. "I think we should go in the other room to play so Michael doesn't wake up." Michael settled down and slept peacefully between them again. Susan put her dolls aside and tiptoed into the kitchen to get Michael's bottle. Vinnie stopped playing and watched her. A sound from the stairwell faintly disturbed him. Did he hear footsteps? Or was he imagining them? No it was footsteps, not Evie's. Not Grandpa Will's. Not the strange men's either. They were his father's footsteps, drunken footsteps, heavy stumbling footsteps. Susan heard them too and froze at the door, her hand clenched Michael's bottle like a weapon. She looked to Vinnie who held his finger to his lips in a silent shush.

"Evie!" Alek pounded at the door and yelled, "Evie, open the door!" Vinnie mimed for Susan to pick up Michael and go into the other room. Susan protested then picked up Michael and defiantly sat on the couch, although she was trembling, she was not going to leave Vinnie alone. Vinnie hugged the wall as he neared the door, the whole time his fingers to his lips to remind Susan to be quiet.

"Vinnie. Don't..." Susan mouthed. She thought Vinnie intended to open the door.

"Shh!" Vinnie said aloud.

"I heard you Evie. Open the damn door," Alek shouted and pounded in a familiar beat that Vinnie recalled from their old house. Evie would lock herself in the bathroom after an argument and Alek would pummel and hammer on the door until Evie opened it.

"Dad?"

"Vinnie?"

"She's at work."

"Open the door Vinnie."

"She's at work. She just left."

"She's not at work. I was just there. Open the door Susan."

"Susan and the others are asleep. Dad, Ma told me not to open the door – for anyone."

"Open the goddamn door."

"Dad, I gotta go to bed. I have to be in bed by nine."

"Open the door Vinnie. Your mom she's not at work...."

"Dad please — I have to go to bed."

"No, you have to open this goddam door. She's not at work."

Then they heard Alek slump to the floor, his head hit the door jamb with a loud thud. Understanding the storm had passed, Susan tiptoed with Michael in her arms into the bedroom. Vinnie's insides rose then sank as he slid down the door to the floor. His head rested on the door jamb just like his father's. The two males, the older, and the younger, in the brewing dark, waited for Evie to come home.

CHAPTER ELEVEN

On Monday morning, Howard had been slow to wake as he fought to keep the lingering images of Evie from fading away when he opened his eyes. As he lay in bed, he devised a plan to ask Sister Mary to schedule an appointment with Evie. He would tell her the meeting would be to provide Mrs. Korli with an update on Vinnie's spiritual counseling. He would have to remember to call Evie, Mrs. Edwards when he gave Sister Mary the instruction he thought as he attached his clerical collar to his black shirt. He had been taking his collar off and on so much lately but he disliked the thought of wearing a cassock all the time.

When Howard arrived at school he stopped by Sister Mary's office but found Sister Veronica instead. She held her hand up, and signaled Howard to wait, "Yes, Chancellor Brennan, I understand. Yes. I will make the necessary arrangements," Sister Veronica said into the phone as Howard surveyed the room for an adult place to sit. There in the corner was the demerit chair. The stiff-backed chair behind her desk was certainly off limits. Howard chose to lean against the wall, his arms folded neatly at his chest. Sister Veronica was one of the younger nuns at St. Anthony's. She was sturdy and tall and a bit stooped, her hands were often clasped at her waist as if she practiced being a nun her whole life. Even her face was nun-like, and if Howard was ever to see her without her habit, which was highly unlikely, he would have thought her a nun just the same. Sister Veronica hung up the phone, turned ever so slightly towards Howard, as if to avoid looking at him directly, "That was the Chancellor; Bishop McKenna will be here tomorrow!"

"I've never met the Bishop."

"I have! We have a lot of work to do to prepare. The Chancellor said he was coming to visit Father Murphy and would like to visit the school while he was here."

"Father Murphy? He hadn't mentioned it to me."

"Oh, I am sure there's a good reason," Sister Veronica said, her hands unclasped and flitted about in nervousness, "I must get to Sister Catherine's office and tell her. We need to send a note home to be sure the children are dressed properly, and then to the janitor's office to be sure…" Howard interrupted, "Sister, I was just stopping by to look for Sister Mary, have you seen her?"

"She was just here a moment ago, oh and I need…," Howard interrupted again, "I will just leave her a note then and be off to find Father Murphy to see if there is anything I can do to help prepare for the Bishop's visit." Howard wrote a quick note asking Sister Mary to schedule a meeting with Evie. He wrote that it was not urgent, but important. Sister Veronica had already run off when the phone rang again. Howard answered it.

"Hello, St. Anthony's School," said Howard.

"This is Chancellor Brennan calling for Sister Veronica."

"She was just called away, may I help you? This is Father Russo."

"Oh, yes Father Russo. Father Murphy has spoken of you just recently. You've been with St. Anthony's just over a year now."

"Yes, Chancellor. It has gone by fast. A wonderful community here but a lot of need too."

"Yes, yes. Well, I don't mean to be rude, but, I only have a minute. I was just calling to let Sister Veronica know that Bishop McKenna also would like a list of the names of the parishioners."

"Yes, okay, I wrote it down and will be sure to give it to her."

Howard felt this was an odd request and one that somehow made his stomach quail. Evie's name will be on the list, of course, but why did this cause him concern, he thought as he tried to collect his wits.

"Thank you Father Russo, I'm sure the Bishop will be pleased to make your acquaintance tomorrow. Good day," said the Chancellor.

"Of course, yes, looking forward to meeting Bishop McKenna as well," Howard said, not confident that this would be true and that in some way he was being blindsided.

He suddenly had become aware that his collar was crooked, it jutted into his Adam's apple at an uncomfortable angle. As he straightened his collar, he felt a seriousness emanating from the phone, a senseless fate that was yet to be discovered. Howard, pushed his hair back, adjusted his glasses on his face, then carefully placed the message from the Chancellor to Sister Veronica under a paperweight of children skating on a pond, the snow drifted up, then down, and finally settled to the bottom of the icy blue globe as Howard left the room and closed the door.

Before he went to look for Father Murphy, Howard stopped at the men's room to check that his collar was in fact straight, and to gain his composure. The call with the Chancellor still shook him, a quiet unease had seeped into his jaw bone. He stroked and kneaded the side of his face to unleash the tension that had crept towards his temples. Howard stood in front of the mirror, his teeth clenched, his bowels were noisy and full. Why hadn't Father Murphy told him of the Bishop's visit? Why? The Howard in the mirror didn't look like the Howard he knew. The mirror no longer reflected the compassionate, gentle face he had inherited from his father, instead the reticent, worried face of his mother stared back at him. His eyes darted about like hers, and as if she was standing behind him he heard the hush hush sound she made whenever he spoke of a discomfort or need. Howard, hush hush. "Our Father," Howard prayed, "strike me down if Father Murphy knows of my deeds. Strike me down." And again, Howard heard the hush hush from his mother's lips, her never ending fear that he would bring unwanted attention to himself. Howard felt a rush of heat to his face, a tightening in his knees that prevented him from moving. He splashed some water on his face, looked once more into the mirror, "Please God, please help me," he whispered, then dried his face and went to look for Father Murphy.

Howard found Father Murphy sweeping the front steps of the school. His back was hunched, as he pushed the broom across one step, then down to the next step. Something in his precision made Howard wonder what it would feel like to take him by the shoulders and shake him. How could Father Murphy not have told him about the Bishop's visit? Why had he left him out of the preparations? Father Murphy was usually intolerable to be around, and now this. Howard also feared that Father Murphy may have become aware of his visits to Dell's and his interest in Evie. Or did he know that Howard had been helping himself to the collection plate each Sunday, ciphering off a few hundred dollars here and there to give to Evie. Father Murphy looked up, his gray eyes squinted to see Howard.

"Pardon me Father," Howard stammered. Father Murphy unsettled him so easily.

"What is it Howard?" Father Murphy inspected the stairs, saw a lone frayed leaf and pushed it into the pile.

"Sister Veronica mentioned that the Bishop was visiting tomorrow. I was wondering if there was anything I could do to help with preparations.

"Of course, of course, I've been remiss in not mentioning the visit to you, but I didn't want you to worry. The Bishop will usually surprise a new priest at their office, a kind of inspection so to speak. Sometimes the new priests get so worked up with too much advance notice that the meeting does not go well," Father Murphy explained.

"Thank you for your thoughtfulness, I had no idea of such a meeting or inspection," Howard said, steadying his voice despite the unease he felt once again in the pit of his stomach.

"Yes, after a year or so, the Bishop wants to be sure you are comfortable and that you are offered the opportunity to discuss any personal or professional issues you may have. And to offer confession as well, especially since it is often difficult for new priests to maintain a healthy confession practice with their supervisor, that being me of course. I have noticed your absence in the confessional," Father Murphy replied with a heaviness that deepened Howard's unease. This was bound to happen sooner or later Howard thought. How could he have been so stupid to think that his misdeeds would go unnoticed? Did he think Father Murphy a fool? If it had to be a choice between his love for Evie and her children and his love for Church, why shouldn't he let Father Murphy know of his personal suffering? Father Murphy was meant to be his mentor, his guide. Howard had failed him. And now the Bishop was coming to meet him and expected to hear his confession. Father Murphy was right to not have mentioned the visit to him, his anxiety had grown exponentially just in the past few minutes.

"Father, I will be prepared for the visit, I hope not to let you down," Howard said.

"How could you let me down? Father, you have had an exemplary year and you are well-liked in our little community." Howard wasn't sure how to respond, so he took the broom from Father Murphy and continued sweeping.

"Let me finish this up for you. It's the least I can do," Howard said and hoped the physical movement of sweeping would shore up his nerves.

"Thank you, Father. Try not to worry, I'm sure your meeting will go well. Just be yourself." Father Murphy's usual terseness had softened and for a moment Howard felt that possibly he had misjudged him, perhaps Father Murphy had his best interest in mind.

After he finished sweeping Howard tended to his pear tree, feeling still more profoundly disconcerted than composed. A small hair ribbon lay in the dirt; it was a shade of light blue that reminded Howard of the small blue suitcase he had packed just a year ago.

The sexton had laid the blue suitcase on his bed while he was at breakfast. He felt a quiet deep joy that he had eaten his last breakfast of stale bread, bruised apples, and poached eggs. Seven undershirts, seven pairs of briefs, seven pairs of black socks, seven black shirts, and two pairs of black pants fit snuggly under his surplice. Howard had shut the suitcase and locked it.

The case was surprisingly light as he walked down the hallway toward the door. The same two frail priests, Father Dominic and Father Bernard, who had greeted him ten years earlier stood on either side. The old priests breathed heavily in concert, although Howard had aged, they seemed to have not. The shorter of the two priests, Father Dominic, rested his hand on Howard's shoulder, while Father Bernard placed a wooden cross around his neck. Howard stooped and bowed his head. Both of the priests' shoes had mud caked around the soles. He wondered if they had been in the garden or the orchard.

The trees. His trees. What would happen to the pear trees he had planted his first summer here? On Howard's second day at the Seminary he had forgotten to make his bed. He was sent out to work in the orchard as his punishment. Father Joseph had ordered five hundred trees to be set in the new clearing. The boys who had forgotten to make their beds, or chewed too loudly, or mumbled their prayers had cleared the land the year before. Now the new sinners would plant an orchard.

In the early mornings Howard worked alongside Father Joseph and the sexton. They dug holes with pointed shovels, snipped burlap, and unwrapped roots before wedging the saplings down into the pooled water at the bottom of each hole. Howard was drawn into quietude as he scraped and prodded the dirt around the roots. When the dirt was good and almost packed, Howard and the sexton tamped any loose soil under their heavy boots, leaving their foot prints at the base of each sapling like a signature.

The pear trees produced fruit in just two years instead of the typical four. Father Joseph and Howard were sure it was because of their habitual watering in the early mornings when the air still had a sober mystery and before the sun cracked through the small recessed windows of their tiny bedrooms. Howard knew not to show too much attachment to his trees as it would be sign of pride that would not be tolerated. In his ten years at the Seminary, he had come to love those trees, and the peaceful dark times when he carried buckets of pale water to them each morning. The trees were Howard's anchor, where the gentle and silent nature in him was protected and useful. It was in the orchard that Howard truly believed in

God. He came to understand that the men inside the Seminary were not students of Jesus's teachings of love and peace, instead they were masters of fear and betrayal.

Father Dominic squeezed Howard's arm and pressed an envelope into his hand. Father Bernard priest blessed him and opened the door. Both priests bowed as Howard stumbled out into full morning sun, its long splintered rays streamed over the green pears ripening for the next harvest. His trees. The hush of his orchard rushed through his flesh for the last time.

A nun, wearing a cross larger than Howard's waved from a royal blue Cadillac for Howard to get in. Howard had dismissed the rumors about what happened when it was your time to leave the seminary. There were fantastic stories about having to walk thirty miles to the nearest town and take a bus, or hitch a ride on a passing wagon driven by an Amish farmer, or that the Bishop himself came to pick you up and drove you to your destination. Your destination also become the subject of much reverie, so much so that the seminarians were forbidden to discuss it with anyone. For, of course, it was God's will where you were to serve him, and having any hopes or wishes about a specific location or quality of life was sinful. Who were you to ask God where you should serve? He would tell you.

Howard's surprise that a nun was to deliver him to his destination was clearly marked on his face. The nun's face was open and cheerful but fell into a solemn look as if to model how he should look. Howard closed his mouth, set his eyes straight ahead, clutched the envelope, and waited.

"I'm Sister Anne," she said as took the envelope from his hand and opened it, "let's see where you are headed."

"Thank...," Howard stopped, his words slipped back down his throat when he saw the wad of cash that Sister Anne removed from the envelope. There was a note too, with the address of his first parish. His flock waited for him at St. Anthony's Church in Albany. Sister Anne removed a wallet from her handbag. She placed the money in the fold. A plastic cover lined the edges of his social security card on one side and a picture of Jesus on the other. She handed him the wallet and the note.

"God bless you Father."

"God bless you Sister."

The next morning, Bishop McKenna took up the entire doorway to Howard's office. His large frame filled his black cassock trimmed with red cord and finished with matching silk-covered buttons. His shoulder cape touched the edges of the door jamb. A red silk skull cap barely covered his equally big head. The traditional green and metallic gold cord of his pectoral cross was affixed to a gold festoon which swung outward as he walked through the door and raised his hand out to Howard. Howard knelt and kissed the Bishop's jeweled ring. It was decorated with raised Celtic tracery and a round amethyst. Up close it looked like a real amethyst and at least 24 karat gold, Howard thought as he rose to his feet and felt his collar to be sure it was straight.

"Father Russo, let us have a chat," Bishop McKenna said rather unceremoniously. His voice was surprisingly nasal with a hint of Brooklyn accent.

"Of course," Howard replied and offered the Bishop the chair in front of his desk, "please have a seat."

Bishop McKenna walked around the desk and sat in Howard's chair. He shifted the papers and the pencils to the side and leaned in on his elbows, his cheeks blazed as he smugly said, "Sit." Howard did as he was told.

"This diocese was established in 1847. It covers 10,419 square miles in fourteen counties, with a total population of 330,000 parishioners that attend 127 parishes. I have 106 active priests and 90 retired priests. A bishop is to have a special concern for their priests. We listen to them. We ensure that they are adequately provided for in every way. This is my job. And today, I have come to do my job."

Howard tried hard not to fidget in his seat. He remained still, his hands firmly clasped on his thighs as if his very life depended on it.

"Yes, Bishop. Thank you," Howard said, a noticeable energy of danger and surprise filled the room.

"The Devil is everywhere, Father Russo. Everywhere. Have you seen the Devil? Has he come to visit you this year?"

"Bishop, I'm not sure what is happening."

"Is that so?" said the Bishop as he leaned in a little closer, his mouth terse, lips puckered as he pensively swayed his head.

"I think you know exactly what is happening. Let us begin your confession."

"But we're not in the confessional," Howard said, aware that it didn't matter but bided for time to think. At that moment, there was knock on the door. The Bishop's eyes barely moved, "Come in." Vinnie stepped into the room. Howard turned to see Vinnie holding a note.

"Can I help you son?" the Bishop said, his eyes turned gleefully towards Vinnie.

"Sister Mary asked me to bring this to Father Russo," Vinnie said and held the note up for the Bishop to see.

"Read it aloud," demanded the Bishop.

Vinnie looked at Father Russo for permission. A mistake.

"Son, read it aloud," the Bishop demanded again.

Vinnie looked to Howard one more time. Howard nodded, another mistake. Bishop McKenna rose from the desk, stood in front of Vinnie and boxed his ears. As he pulled his hands back the sun lit up his gold band. Howard gasped with astonishment as Vinnie defiantly looked up at the Bishop, unyielding to the pain he must have felt. The Bishop reached out and boxed his ears again, Vinnie looked to Howard again this time his eyes were wet with pain.

"Are you deaf young man? I said read the note."

Vinnie opened the note, his speech halted, but determined, "Dear Father Russo, Mrs. Korli will be available tomorrow after school to meet with you."

"Who is Mrs. Korli?" the Bishop demanded of Vinnie again.

"My mother," Vinnie replied and looked at the floor.

"Your mother. Now why does your mother need to meet with Father Russo?"

"Father has been counseling me so I can be good."

"Is that so?"

The Bishop turned toward Howard now, "Perhaps this young man is a good candidate for the Seminary. What do you think Father? The chiding in his voice revealed a ferocious joy that Howard had encountered when he was a boy. The timbre and volume of the voice that provoked an uncertainty as to what was the correct thing to say to avoid further humiliation.

"Vinnie is the eldest of four, he is needed at home," Howard said and hoped that this answer would satisfy the Bishop and release Vinnie. Instead, his answer prompted the Bishop to ask Vinnie more questions.

"Why are you needed at home?"

"My father left. I have to help care for my brother and sisters."

"That's a big responsibility for a young boy. Do you have time for your studies?"

"Yes," Vinnie said. Howard was impressed with the way Vinnie handled the Bishop. He understood the evil in this man as well as Howard.

"Bishop, Sister Mary told me to come right back."

The Bishop held out his hand to Vinnie. Vinnie was not sure what to do. The Bishop pushed him to his knees, and placed his ring in Vinnie's face.

"Kiss the ring."

Vinnie kissed the ring. The amethyst looked like a girl's ring to Vinnie as his lips touched the rose-colored rock.

"You are dismissed."

Vinnie rose. His knees shook as he left the room. He didn't turn back, He didn't hop down the stairs two at time. He didn't run his hands along the lockers. He walked solemnly towards the boys room, his ears rung with pain, he saw only black as he closed the stall door, the spasms he had suppressed came out in a whimper at first, then a feeling of great despair for himself, and for Father Russo as his whole body shook and released the pain from his jaw. His lips burned with the humiliation of kissing the ring on the stupid lard ass Bishop's white pudgy finger. The deep hate he had held only for his father, was now conjoined with his hate for the Bishop. This hate of men in authority rooted so deep in Vinnie's heart that when he grew up he didn't recognize it as hate—or call it hate—instead it manifested into a strike first behavior—Vinnie's every action was governed by his chance to humiliate before being humiliated.

The Bishop started in again as soon as Vinnie left the room.

"Where were we? Ah yes, your confession? Is there something about Mrs. Korli you would like to tell me? Women are the Devil's helpers you know." Howard knew the Bishop was taunting him, yet still he was confused by his apparent animosity.

"By this time you must be aware of the effect of your good looks on the women in the Parish. Father Murphy has noted it in your file. He also noted that there appears to be money missing each week from the collection baskets that you are in charge of. Shall I continue or would you like to help me understand things bit better?"

"I...I... am not sure where to start."

"Well why don't you think it over while I visit with Father Murphy? Oh and Father Russo, Father Bohr sends his regards. He's an old friend. We were in Seminary together. I wasn't surprised at all when I learned he went back to Immaculate Conception Seminary. He was always fond of mentoring and teaching the new boys," Bishop McKenna said as he rifled through Howard's desk, opening and slamming the drawers shut. He pulled out Howard's bible, laid it on the desk.

"This is where your bible belongs. Not in the drawer. When I return tomorrow morning, I expect to see this bible here in one hand and the money you borrowed from the collection basket in the other."

"Yes, Bishop," Howard said, so aware of the Bishop's deception and ill will that he wanted to punch him in the face, strangle him with his pectoral cross, shove his 24 karat gold ring down his throat until he choked and gasped for his very last breath. What the Bishop had done to Vinnie, the damage, the humiliation was more than Howard could bear, it was as if the Bishop hurt his own son, his own flesh and blood. The sickness of violence towards the Bishop seeped through Howard's bloodstream. He felt so very alone, so alone, just as Vinnie did standing before the Bishop, his ears boxed, his power taken. The Bishop and Father Bohr were old friends; now his visit made perfect sense.

Howard ignored the Bishop's request. He composed himself as best he could then walked toward the gymnasium. As soon as he saw that a team of boys waited for him, eager to play basketball, eager to be part of something bigger then themselves, he was able to completely shake the Bishop from his thoughts.

Howard was pleased to see the ten boys who showed up for the basketball try outs. And he was relived and surprised to see Vinnie was there, shuffling his feet in place as the other boys horsed around. Howard approached Vinnie casually, so as not to draw the attention of the other boys, "Vinnie, you okay, son?" Vinnie wouldn't make eye contact but nodded his head slightly and then ran off to the sideline, retrieved a ball, and flung it with all his might across the gymnasium toward the hoop.

The practice had been going quite well until Howard tripped on his cassock as he swiped at a ball headed for out of bounds. Down on the floor, Howard recalled his darkest secret. The fluorescent lights of the dingy, ill lit gym, the flickering bulbs of a cold yellow light pushed Howard into a state of confusion. It was if he had had a stroke. Howard lay on the floor oblivious to the boys surrounding him, shouting "Are you alright?" "Should we get help?"

Howard just lay there, covered in sweat, in the middle of that smoky, caliginous, room. The room was buried deep in the complex, beyond the cells for the boys, beyond the sunlit rooms of the priests, even beyond the orchards. The boys were driven there by the sexton. Awakened in the time *between evening and morning*, the sexton entered their room with a candle and beckoned them to come with him. Boy after boy was taken to The Sanctuary, where old priests waited for the new recruits; each boy unaware that he was already spoken for. Howard's initiation was with Father Bohr — Bohr, the perfect name for the bulky, massively built predator that he was.

The first time Howard was awakened by the sexton, he was driven to the interior of the Seminary in a black Mercury Monterey, its huge steering wheel shined in the moonlight. Howard went from barely awake to high alert and demanded to know where he was being taken. The sexton turned slightly, his voice bound with anguish, "To see Father Bohr. Best to be quiet."

Howard started to speak again, this time the sexton cut him off with a loud and terse, "Quiet!"

Howard had never seen a car that had just two leather seats and a gold winged hood ornament. The ornament reminded him of angel wings; of a passage of St. John Vianney he had read earlier that week. St. John wrote that if a person was to meet a priest and an angel, they should salute the priest before they salute the angel. The latter is the friend of God; but the priest holds His place.

Further in the passage, St. John asked, "What is a priest?" His answer surprised and comforted Howard. St. John wrote that a priest is a man who holds the place of God — a man who is invested with all the powers of God. And this seemed to Howard to be something he wanted, and that his parents had wanted for him; to be invested with all the powers of God.

The sexton opened the car door and guided Howard toward what he would come to learn was called The Sanctuary. He was now fully awake. A fear he had never experienced stopped him cold. The sexton patted him on the back as if to reassure him, but it only caused Howard more panic. He tried to turn back but the sexton put a strong hold on the back of his neck and walked him toward a large shingled house. An ordinary looking house except for the door. It had a shuttered window with a wooden cross to hold the panels together. The sexton knocked once then twice, then twisted the wooden cross and opened the shutters. Father Bohr's face appeared, he nodded, and opened the door.

The sexton, released his hold on Howard's neck as Father Bohr extended his hand to Howard and led him inside. As the door closed behind them, he heard a boy screaming, horrifying screams, pain-filled screams that demanded attention. Father Bohr led him down a hallway, the floor boards creaked beneath their feet, the boy had stopped screaming. There were other sounds now, rhythmic sounds, like someone opening and shutting a drawer. Grunts. Heavy breaths.

As they neared a staircase, Howard legs stopped working. Father Bohr's silence, his strong grip on Howard's hand, the sounds, the awful sounds, brought on a paralysis, one that seemed familiar to Father Bohr. He scooped Howard up into his arms and carried him up the stairs, over the threshold into a bedroom like a bride, and placed him on a bed. Before the door closed, Howard saw across the hall, two pairs of bare legs intertwined, a boy turned, it was Paul, he was a year ahead of him, he was sitting on top of a man moving up and down, up and down, his eyes closed when he saw Howard looking at him. On a cabinet in the corner a stereo played a familiar opera.

Howard recognized it from music class, Dance of the Seven Veils from Strauss's Salome. He recalled Father Tom had discussed at great length the part when the severed head of John the Baptist is unveiled. The turntable hissed, the cicadas screeched into the chilling pitch-black darkness outside the window, the bed springs groaned as Father Bohr settled himself next to Howard.

In the morning the boys were led to the shower by the sexton, he had also brought them clean clothes. After they were dressed, the sexton gave them a hunk of bread and a canteen of water, but didn't offer them a ride back to the Seminary, instead Paul motioned for Howard to follow him. They headed down a dirt path on the east side of the orchard, the sky overhead burned blue by the sun. Its rays illuminated the trees, revealing the pears were just shadows of themselves, the small green ovals hanging from their branches. As the boys' feet scraped along the path, the faint scent of pine further woke their senses, Paul reached out, put a hand on Howard's shoulder, and disrupted his sober gait.

"It won't be your turn again for a while," Paul said. He looked Howard in the eye for the first time. Howard bent over and retched, a foamy yellow bile dripped from his chin. Paul wiped Howard's face tenderly with his shirttail, tore the hunk of bread in half and gave it to Howard. Howard took a bite, a sip of water, and the two boys walked in silence as they circled the orchard, went down the hill, through the pine forest, across the great lawn, then up the path to the open Seminary doors.

Howard stepped through the doors, a different boy, a bruised and sore boy; a boy who wouldn't understand how much he had lost until he was a very old man, in a very old chair, on a damp and raw day, mourning the person he had not become. In his wrinkled pajamas, and stocking feet, Howard would stare out a window in his small room at Opus Bono Sacerdotii, a hospice for old priests. He would remember that rawboned, enthusiastic, boy who had entered the seminary, so compact and slim at just twelve years old. The braveness of his earlier self, standing at the door to the Seminary, his father proud of his sacrifice, his offering of his youngest son to the Church. That boy, the one his father loved and kindled, the innocent boy who saluted his father before he passed through the Seminary doors, the Howard that his father knew, had died there. The Howard he had become, was born to Father Bohr, a thief and a beast.

"Hey Father Russo? Father Russo! Should we get help?" Vinnie said, standing over him, still holding the ball.

"No, no, I'm fine. Just a bit clumsy today," Howard replied, stood and brushed off his cassock. Vinnie bounced the ball toward him, Howard caught it, feigned a pass to Vinnie then shot a basket from the half court line. Vinnie and the other boys' mouths fell open as the ball swooshed through the net.

The next morning when Howard arrived at his office Father Murphy sat in his chair instead of the Bishop. It had been a long night, in fact, Howard had not slept at all. He had paced the floor of his bedroom for several hours admonishing himself for his stupidity. He tried to compose a written confession but the list got longer and longer, and finally he tore it to shreds then burned it in his trash can. When he did try to close his eyes to rest, he couldn't fend off the image of Bishop McKenna boxing Vinnie's ears. An anger, unmatched by any other anger he felt in his entire life, collapsed his lungs and caused him to choke on his own spit when he thought of how casually Bishop McKenna uttered Father Bohr's name. How stupid he was to think that he could escape those evil men, and how unbelievably naive he had been to even mildly trust Father Murphy.

"Father Murphy, I was expecting the Bishop."

"Yes, I know."

"Will I still meet with him?"

"No. He left yesterday after our meeting. He is confident that I can provide the guidance you need."

"Yes, Father."

"You see, there are rules that I am sure they taught you at Seminary. Those rules and the people are the same here, things are no different, we must only rely on one another to insure we are protected," Father Murphy leaned in just as the Bishop had done, "Do you understand me?"

"Not quite Father. I did take the money, and I am having feelings for Mrs. Korli, and I have been drinking, and I have lied to you and to my parishioners, and…."

"That's enough Father Russo. You are a man, and like any man, we keep our money matters and physical needs private. You will be expected to do the same and not call any attention to yourself. Am I clearer to you now?"

"Yes, Father."

"For example, Mrs. Fletcher is the one who noticed the money missing and brought it to my attention. You mustn't be so stupid. If you need money there's money, if you need a woman, do so, but quietly, if you need other things that some men need, do them other places, not here in our home.

Priests are men. Men are animals, and animals don't shit where they eat. Remember this and you and I will continue to get along just fine."

With that, Father Murphy flipped open the bible on Howard's desk, inside was a stack of bills. He shut the book and threw it on Howard's lap.

"I'll expect you to keep our Church in good standing with the Bishop. He only has so much patience for ignorantia affectata, your conspicuously cultivated ignorance is even too much for me. If it continues, you will find yourself a prisoner of the compromises you have made; the dishonesty you have engaged in, the hypocrisy, these things are terrible burdens we all face, but trying to maintain intellectual and spiritual integrity while attending to the needs of being a mere human will lead you to despair. Accept that we all bend the rules quietly, and you will stay closer to the truth than if you don't," Father Murphy said as he shut the door to Howard's office.

"Yes Father," Howard said to the closed door, "Yes."

Howard turned from the door and sunk his face into his hands as shame trembled through his body. He closed his eyes and wished for death. Father Murphy and the Bishop's actions should no longer puzzle him, yet they did. After a little while it occurred to Howard that his disgust had always been present, yet he chose, as Father Murphy so aptly observed, to ignore it. When did he first have these feelings? He remembered. The memory was so real, as if he was a boy again.

The car was silent. Howard watched his mother, Maria. She had sat in the front seat, her Sunday veil pinned to her hat, and said her rosary. Howard's breath was shallow, suppressed, each exhale was blocked by the cigar smoke that had filled the car. His father, Salvatore, looked in the rear view mirror, sighed, and cracked the window. Howard's asthma often dampened his father's pleasure of smoking, which became the case as they rode alongside a dense wood, on a winding dirt road, to the top of a hill. There a Romanesque Revival building stood, the seminary. The Immaculate Conception Seminary was four stories of glowing pastel brick and sat on a sweep of green lawn above a deep blue pond. Howard adjusted his coat. He spit on his shoes and rubbed them on his pant leg. He straightened his tie. The car came to a full stop. There was nothing else for him to do.

His father opened the trunk and handed him his bag. His mother held her rosary to her lips. Howard and Salvatore walked the brick path to the seminary door. They stopped. Two old priests flanked the entryway, each turned and shook his father's hand. Salvatore straightened Howard's tie, rubbed his hand over Howard's cheek, his palm briefly held Howard's chin as he looked deep in his boy's eyes, proud. Howard, startled by the bold intensity of his father's goodbye, felt his heart pulse, and his breath shortened again. He loved his father and his father loved him. The rasps that vibrated from Howard's nostrils were now clogged with tears. His father drew him to his chest. His strong arms wrapped tightly across Howard's back. Wrapped. Howard shrank into his father's embrace, hushed, silent, and accepting.

The defined arch of the entry way into the seminary felt far away, his father drew him near once more then let go, a release into the unknown, a release that Howard would later come to understand was his father's faith in God, in those who served Him, and in this honorable and difficult decision to sacrifice his youngest son to the priesthood. His father's footsteps fell flat against the pale brick as he headed toward the car, his hands in his front pocket, his head bent slightly downward. Howard wanted to run after him and his father must have sensed it. Salvatore turned at the end of the path, raised his hand, his strong wide palms turned downward touched his forehead briefly and saluted his son.

Howard raised his own hand, the sun splintered around his father, a glistening halo of colors and white light enveloped his father as Howard touched the tip of his index finger to his own forehead, and thrust his hand into the air. The sun, now shielded from his eyes, the halo and white light dissipated, Howard and Salvatore stood solid, the light now opaque and hazy, until they both released their hands to their sides. The priests nodded for Howard to enter. The car motor faded as the heavy wooden doors closed.

CHAPTER TWELVE

"Evie. You said the sitter was coming to get them soon. That was frigging three hours ago," Stan hissed sharply.

Evie carefully tied and retied her apron, hoping her silence would calm Stan down.

"And your ex-husband was here again looking for you. He was here last week too. I had to tell him you weren't here again! I hope he isn't going to be a problem."

"Alek? He was here again."

Evie tried to suppress her unease; she tied and retied her apron a second time.

"That's what I just said. This is getting too complicated. Things need to be simpler Evie, they just need to be. You gonna stand there retying your apron all night or get to work?"

"I'm sorry Stan, I don't know what is going on with him. He showed up at my place last week and scared the kids bad. He told them I wasn't at work when I was just late," Evie's voice choked.

"Hey, what am I supposed to do? You're not here, you're not here. I can't say you're here. The guy's not stupid you know, if your car ain't out there, how can I say you're here."

"I'm really sorry. I'll try to talk to him."

"Forget Alek, the other girls are gonna be all over me 'bout this."

"Vinnie had a game. He'll be here soon."

"What? You gonna let him drive them home?"

"No, of course not, and my car is in the shop anyway. I'll call a cab and take five."

"No you won't Evie. First, I'm your nanny and now you're gonna take five?"

"Well then he'll wait with them while I finish the shift. Your choice," Evie replied with a firmness and hoped Stan would say no more. Susan twirled her hair and looked at Stan. Stan looked at her then Evie then back to Susan.

"Last time Evie. The other girls — I don't even want to go near them tonight."

Evie scampered out while Stan sat down and pulled out his ledger. He docked an hour of her time. Not taking food from her children's mouths, but a clear message, he tried to reason as he looked over at JoBeth sleeping soundly next to Michael on a blanket on the floor. He erased the mark in the ledger and sighed. Evie would always have her way with me, Stan thought, and put the ledger away. Susan had opened the second drawer of his desk and took out a deck of cards, dealt Stan a hand, and then stared at him.

"You shouldn't stare at people, it's rude."

"You're not people, you're Stan."

"What are we playing?"

"Blackjack."

"Blackjack eh? What do you know about blackjack?"

"I know I can win. I beat my Daddy and Emil all the time. I also pick the horse that wins."

"So you say."

"Susan, shush. Don't tell family secrets," Vinnie said. He dropped his gym bag to the floor; startling Michael for a moment.

"Basketball?" Stan asked.

"Guard, wanted to be Center but not tall enough."

"You got time," Stan said, and dealt Vinnie a hand.

Evie poked her head in the room, and saw the five of them, two of her children sleeping and two playing cards with her friend Stan. Evie realized her resentment of their indifference to her presence before she spoke up. She was working so hard as they enjoyed the benefits of her labor without the realization of the urgency of their situation, that she had one chance toward betterment and that was her dependency on a priest for tips. Surely she would burn in hell, but her children wouldn't be deprived of all the things that would lead to their advancement. Evie touched each of their faces, lingering at Michael's. She was appreciative of his curly brown hair as soft as a lamb's belly.

"Stan, I gave the girls my tips for the night. They won't bother you."

Stan nodded and dealt Susan another card after she said, "Hit me." Stan raised an eyebrow at Vinnie before unveiling a Jack of Diamonds.

"Vinnie, it'll just be another half hour or so. Things are winding down."

When Evie got back to her station, Leo was there.

"Look who's here to see you."

Howard was at the bar studying the menu. Evie was not in the least angry with Leo for pointing out that he knew Father Russo's intentions. What perplexed her was that neither man was capable of revealing their true feelings to her. The harder Leo tried to pretend he didn't like her, the more he did, and the more she didn't like him. And inversely the more Howard pretended to not like her, the more he liked her, and the more she liked him. Then there was Stan, who was caring for her children despite the fact that she would never consider loving him.

"Is not!" Evie said a little too loud and caused Father Russo to turn and look at them.

"Father Russo?"

"Hi. I just dropped off Vinnie and thought I'd see if you and the children needed a ride home since you're without a car."

"Thank you. How'd you know my car is in the shop?"

"Vinnie told me on the ride over."

"Thank you Father. Will we all fit in your car? There are five of us you know."

"More than enough room. Take your time. I can certainly keep myself occupied until you are ready."

"I'll just be a few more minutes," Evie called over her shoulder. She dashed to the ladies room. Just as she had always done whenever Father Russo came to dine, she freshened her lipstick, quickly teased her bangs, and checked her stockings for runs. This time though, Evie undid the top two buttons of her uniform, not just the first one. She leaned in toward the mirror to see how much of her chest Father Russo would be able to see when she bent over to serve him.

Before she headed back to the bar, Evie stopped at Stan's office. Vinnie and Susan were fast asleep; their heads rested on Vinnie's gym bag for a pillow. JoBeth was curled up under Stan's desk. Michael lay on his blanket, his eye sockets puffy and frail, his lips slightly parted, his pacifier laid beside him. Evie put the pacifier in Michael's mouth. All she could hear were her own footsteps in the hallway as she returned to the bar. Her knees wobbled a bit as she arrived back at Howard's side as she became increasingly aware that the more nonchalant she tried to be, the more obvious it was that she was trying too hard.

"Ready?" He asked, touching his collar as he stood. He suddenly felt oddly shy and deeply aware of Evie's attempt at normalcy. Did he really believe that she didn't know how he felt about her?

"Well, they're all asleep. Can I get you something?" Evie asked trying to alleviate the look of constraint she saw on Howard's face.

"The usual," Howard replied, and returned to his seat, loosened his shirt at the neck, removed his collar, and put it in his coat pocket.

Evie went behind the bar and attempted to make two martinis. Howard pushed a ten dollar bill across the bar, Evie put it in the tip jar, and came back around the front of the bar. Howard patted the stool next to him and motioned for her to sit. Her long stockinged legs swung from the stool. Howard watched her hands as she picked up her martini and clanked her glass against his. He couldn't help but notice that she hadn't shaken it and that the vermouth had sank to the bottom of the cheap cocktail glass.

"Cheers," Howard said, took a sip, and tried to withhold his disappointment. She had made the martinis with gin; and the bad vermouth over-powered the drink.

"Is the drink okay? You've only taken a sip," Evie asked, sure she had gotten it wrong.

"It's fine. Really quite fine. Not quite expert, but well on your way," Howard said reassuringly.

"I can't thank you enough. I was gonna have to call a cab."

"No problem, really. Vinnie had a great game tonight. He's great on defense."

"That makes sense."

"His father came to the game too."

"Alek?"

"Yes. It seems like he's trying to be a good father."

"Well we'll see, I guess," Evie said, and stood to let Howard know it was time to go. Howard finished up his drink in one gulp, stood, and put his coat on, as he asked, "Shall I help you with the kids?"

"Yes, I'll show you where they are. While you're bringing the car around, I'll pack up. Team work!" Evie said as she walked towards the hallway to Stan's office. She turned and motioned for Howard to follow her. Stan was surprised to see Howard in his office helping Evie with the kids. Stan raised an eyebrow at Evie, but said nothing.

Howard and Evie took turns bringing each child to their bed and watching the car. Howard carried JoBeth up to the apartment first and gently laid her on a small mattress near the wall. JoBeth woke, ever so slightly as Howard tucked a cotton blanket under her chin. JoBeth sat up, her face groggy with sleep and half-finished dreams, and saluted him. Howard raised his hand to his forehead and returned a salute, as he heard the soft thumping and creaking of Evie's footsteps on the stairs. Howard flicked on the nightlight, and returned to the car to retrieve Susan. He passed Evie on the staircase with Michael swaddled in his waffle blanket, her face pressed close to his, murmuring a lullaby, her voice surprisingly deep and husky. Last was Vinnie, Evie half carried and walked him up the staircase. The full weight of his body slumped against Evie's; his untied shoelace dragged behind them. Howard feared they would trip and fall but Evie guided him to his bed patiently self-assured. He woke, like JoBeth, just for a moment.

"I need to say my prayers."

"You can say them twice tomorrow," Evie said, and shepherded him into bed.

Evie walked Howard to the door. An exhaustion swept through her and she leaned against the wall and felt a faint dizziness coming on again.

"Are you okay? You look tired," Howard said tenderly, his hands pushed deep into his pockets, his eyes shifted about, he was afraid to look directly at Evie. He mostly wanted to keep the stillness between them, of the children's slumber, of the quietude of the night that revealed the intimacy that had developed between them, of the fascination he had with all that was yet to be said.

"I'm just so tired. I feel like I'm going to collapse," Evie said as the wall got farther away from her and the vertigo she felt deepened into a panic. She fell into Howard, who had seen her begin to tumble and had wrapped his hands around her waist. He held her briefly until the episode passed, then ushered her to a chair by the door. He knelt beside her and felt her forehead.

"No fever. Do you think a cool cloth will help?" Howard asked.

"Yes, maybe," Evie replied, her eyes watery from the crippling panic she had felt.

Howard let the water run for a good few minutes before he dipped the cloth into the basin. He needed the coolness of the water on his hands to dampen the rushing feelings of exhilaration and joy that pumped through his veins and snapped at his stomach. He had held Evie. He had felt the lovely curve of her waist and the small of her back. His blood flowed so rapidly through him it broke his breath.

"Father Russo, is everything okay?" Evie asked timidly, her voice weakened and apprehensive.

"Be right there," Howard said as he wrung the cloth so hard that the water splattered his shirtsleeves and pants. Evie was not just pale, she was bone white. The cloth he placed on her forehead did nothing to prevent her from fainting. Howard shook her until she finally recovered.

"I'm calling an ambulance," Howard said, firmly, intent on shutting down any resistance.

Too debilitated to protest, Evie blinked, then closed her eyes.

"Please call my mother, she'll take the children," Evie said barely audible.

Howard woke Vinnie to help him. Sleepy-eyed and confused, it took Vinnie a few minutes to understand what Howard was asking of him and for it to become clear as to what was happening to his mother. Vinnie called Will and Doris.

"They'll be here in a few minutes," Vinnie said to Howard as he hung up the phone, "when will the ambulance get here?"

"Soon. Just stay with your sisters and Michael until your grandparents arrive."

"Should I call my Dad?"

"Let your grandparents call, if they think it's best."

"Will my Mom be okay?" Vinnie asked, his face flushed with confusion.

"I think so. She's just tired. She'll be okay."

Doris and Will arrived just as the ambulance drivers had lifted Evie onto the stretcher. Howard assured them he would stay with Evie until they were able to get to the hospital.

When Evie woke the first thing she felt was Howard's hand in hers. His head was thrown back against the top of the chair, his mouth was open as he snored. He had fallen asleep waiting for her to wake. Evie slipped her hand from his and shook him.

"Father Russo. Father Russo, wake up," Evie urged, like a fearful child wakening her sleeping parents.

Howard recognized the voice calling him, a siren, a familiar whisper that soothed and excited him as he woke from a dream where an eerie darkness surrounded him, beckoning him toward a distant ocean alit with silverfish and a boat that gently rocked towards him on listless waves. His eyes finally opened. He was still here, at Evie's bedside. The doctors had come by while she slept and told him Evie had severe anemia and was undernourished. They weren't sure of the cause but she would need to stay in the hospital for at least a couple of days; until her iron was better.

"What happened? I remember standing in the hallway after putting the children to bed."

"You fainted and scared the bejesus out of me," Howard said.

"Where are the children?"

"With your parents. They came by earlier but you were still asleep. The doctor said you have anemia and need to rest for a few days."

"But I have to work tomorrow. And the pups, who has the pups?"

"Your parents took the pups too. I'll stop by Dell's later today and let Stan know you are ill."

"Thank you Father, thank you so much. I really don't know how this happened."

"It doesn't matter, just get some rest, eat, and listen to your doctor. I'll look in on the children, your parents, and even the pups," Howard said, smiling as he took her hand in his again, "Things will be alright, I just know they will. Trust me."

Howard kept his promise to Evie and called on the Edwards often. So often that Will became suspicious of Howard's intentions. Howard was persistent in his offer to look after the children and the pups. Will finally, and emphatically, told Howard that he and his wife were perfectly capable of caring for their family, and that surely there were other parishioners more in need than them. Howard shook Will's hand and said, "Of course, Mr. Edwards. It's just that I made a promise to Evie, and I must be true to my word."

"Well as far as I can see, you have been," Will said, as that same shudder reappeared that he felt when retrieving JoBeth from Father Russo's arms in the Spring. This time it was stronger and more urgent. Father Howard turned to go. He felt Will's eyes on him as he straightened his back, and stifled the urge to run.

Howard fretted for weeks about whether he should visit Evie, or not. The short-term sacrifice, he thought, would yield a greater reward in the long-term. Howard had recited Corinthians 12:4-8 to many wedding couples, but now he, understood, for the first time, the meaning of the words he had so easily spoken: "Love bears all things, believes all things, hopes all things, endures all things." As he remembered these words, he thought himself blessed and privileged to come to a decision so easily. He would forego seeing Evie, and, instead devise a plan to purchase the house.

Howard even considered the idea of asking Leo to help him. He pondered whether perhaps Leo's interest in Evie would be an incentive to want a better life for her. And there was always cash. A tried and true incentive. He would offer Leo one thousand dollars in cash as payment for his help and silence. Howard even went to Dell's one afternoon with the hope of running into Leo again, but as fate would have it, neither he nor Evie were working that day.

Howard then decided to call the realtor just to learn about the process of purchasing the house. He also thought it would be an opportunity to find out if there had been any offers on the house that he had liked. The realtor answered the phone on the second ring.

"Foundry Real Estate, may I help you?"

"Yes, I am calling to inquire about a home in the new development off Route 20," Howard said dryly to cancel his uneasiness.

"Colony Acres?"

"Yes that's the one."

"Which house are you interested in?"

"I think it was 17 Prestige Place."

"Oh yes, that was the developer's favorite as well, the half court is quite a gem," said the man enthusiastically to show he was not fooled by Howard's attempt at disinterest.

"Yes, I thought so as well."

"Oh, you've already seen it?"

"Yes, the inspectors were there when I rode by and offered to show me around. So I took them up on it."

"Excellent, the asking price is thirty six thousand dollars. Would you like to make an offer Mr...? I'm sorry, please excuse me, I didn't introduce myself or get your name. I am Jim Alpert, I've been selling these new homes for the past year or so."

"Of course, this is Mr. — Mr. Korli, my wife and I have been looking for a home for quite a while, she has taken ill and I would like to surprise her. Is it possible to meet this week? It will be a cash purchase, if that is okay?"

"Of course, yes, Mr. Korli, cash is always good. I can send you the paperwork to get started. Where should I send it?"

"I would like to pick it up. Where is your office? You know to get things started sooner rather than later?"

"Why don't we just meet at the house, then you can take another look around, just to be sure. And there are quite a few other homes near completion as well".

"No, no, I like that one. Let's meet there tomorrow."

"Tomorrow it is, sorry your first name was?"

"Howard — Howard Korli, my wife is Evie."

When Howard hung up the phone, the strangeness of the sound of his own voice calling himself another man's name was something he would never overcome. Not that day, nor the day Alek left Evie's life forever, nor the years to come long after he and Evie resided at 17 Prestige Place and had their own child together. Howard had forfeited his own name, relinquished his father's name Russo, and became Howard Korli to live and care for Evie and her children. Of all the things Howard had done, and would do, this act seemed the most unforgivable and perverse of all.

CHAPTER THIRTEEN

The summer had passed before Howard went to Dell's again. He sat at his usual table. The man next to him slurped his soup so loudly that Howard felt conspicuous for him. Howard looked to the man as if to quiet him, but the man gave him a beg-pardon shrug as he placed his spoon by the bowl then reached for the bread basket. Howard wished he could think of something to say when Evie inevitably would appear. He wrung his napkin under the table to release the tension he felt growing in his face and neck. The key in his breast pocket gave him immense yearning and immense doubt. He had taken complete charge of his plan to help Evie and her children and the culmination of his efforts had brought him to this day. This very day, when he packed a small suitcase of clothes and cash and told Mrs. Fletcher he needed to leave town for the night to tend to a sick parishioner, instead he drove to 17 Prestige Place. Inside, he sat on wall-to-wall carpet on the living room floor, his heart quickening with anticipation of the seriousness of the occasion. He tried to hear Evie's voice in his head. Had he forgotten what she sounded like? Over the summer he had seen her at Church and treated her kindly, but provided no hint of his intentions to help her and her children move to a safer neighborhood.

Last Sunday, Evie had appeared with the children wearing that same blue dress she had worn the first time he saw her at Mass, he felt like everyone had watched him watch her. He had wanted to take her in his arms and tell her to wait for him. His thoughts rarely went beyond that, taking her in his arms, because he wasn't quite sure of all the steps from hugging to kissing to making love. He knew he wanted that kind of intimacy with Evie, but how this type of thing actually happened was a mystery. He knew what the old priests at Seminary did to him and the other boys was wrong, yet somehow the wrongness did not dampen his feelings for Evie. In fact, they were very much separate.

Howard was perplexed as to how he would propose his plan to her. He had bought the house and put it in her name. The realtor tried to discourage him, but he made up a story about having to go overseas for work and wanted to keep his estate simple for his ailing wife. The seriousness of what he had done to acquire the home brought Howard to cross himself as he rose from the floor and walked through the house. It felt like a glass bubble with the lights on and no curtains, as if all the world could see his wrongdoing. Even though Father Murphy and Bishop McKenna tacitly condoned his sins, in his heart he didn't want to be like them; one of them. "Dear Heavenly Father, please forgive me for what I have done. What I have stolen will be used to serve a higher purpose. It will provide housing and food for a family who so desperately needs it. Dear Lord in Heaven, I promise, upon my mother's grave, to pay back every cent." Rather than feel forgiven, Howard felt a helpless anguish. What had he done?

Howard heard Evie's heels as they got closer to him but then retreated. Evie had seen Howard as she came out of the kitchen hauling a massive tray for a party of six seated in her station. She stopped in her tracks, turned very slowly so not to drop the tray, and returned to the kitchen. At church he had acted so formal with her that she had convinced herself that the feelings they had exchanged were just sad imaginings. God, she had prayed one night not long ago, please forgive me for having sinful thoughts towards Father Russo. He was probably being kind to me and I mistook his actions as something I shouldn't have. Please forgive me. Amen. But when she saw Howard sitting tall in his chair, expectant as if he was ready to jump out of his seat at the first sight of her, she knew that all had passed between them was real and true.

"Did you forget something?" Arlene asked Evie as she fussed over the tray.

"Uh, no. Can you cover for me? Table 10," Evie's voice trembled. Arlene cocked her head with false concern.

"Sweetie, you okay? You look like you seen a ghost or something."

"Sweetie? Since when do you care Arlene? Really?"

"Whatever, table of six, your loss my gain. And I get the tip!"

"Of course. I'd never expect a favor from you Arlene!"

Arlene mounted the heavy tray onto her shoulder, kicked open the door, and headed to Table 10. Evie peered out through the kitchen door window and saw Howard tilt his head as Arlene approached, then turn slightly until

Arlene was in his peripheral vision, seeing it wasn't her, he picked up his napkin and put it on his lap as if he just arrived.

"Who you looking at?" Max asked.

"Nothing. Just felt a little off and asked Arlene to cover for me. Making sure she does."

"You must feel pretty awful if you had to ask Arlene for help."

"Yeah, kind of."

Evie busied herself with filling bread baskets. She closed her eyes for just a moment. Her thoughts of Father Russo were replaced with thoughts of Vinnie pacing the floors with Michael; of Susan and JoBeth fleeing from a crazy man; of Father Russo holding JoBeth as they said good bye to all the people at church.

"I think the bread baskets are good now Evie. You okay?" Max asked.

Evie hadn't realized she had overfilled half a dozen baskets.

"Yes. Just lost in thought. Best be getting back out there."

Each step Evie took toward Howard's table felt like a sighing of her heart. With her pad in hand, like the first time she waited on him, she greeted him, formally and without yielding to her surprise and relief.

"Father Russo. Nice to see you."

"Nice to see you too Evie. Good to see you at Church last Sunday too. Are you feeling better?" Howard said, matching her formal tone but with a hint of camaraderie.

"I'm better now, thanks," Evie said as she tucked her hair behind her ear, "the usual?"

"No, I had dinner already this evening. Just a martini please. A double though."

"Double. Coming up."

As Howard waited for Evie to return he fidgeted with his table settings.

"Leo, double martini, two olives," Evie called out.

"Look who has returned, the lonely priest," Leo said brazen in his sarcasm.

"What happened to the second one is on me good Catholic bit?"

"There's no hope for me lovely, but there is for you."

"What do you mean by that?"

"Nothing, just take the opportunity to get out of here when it comes around. I missed mine and it looks like this is it, Dell's bartender for life."

"Oh Leo, that's not true and you know it."

"I wish it weren't, but it is. Too many missed chances. Here you go, lovely. Tell Mr. Big Tipper I said hello." Leo had infected Evie with his heaviness. Could this be it? From the deli boy's wife to a waitress at Dell's. She really hadn't made much progress.

"Give me the one on the house, like you always do," Evie demanded of Leo.

"If you think it will help."

"Help what?"

"Don't fight it Evie. The guy is in love with you, and if I weren't in love with you too I would have never seen it coming. He isn't going to keep coming here for free."

"What do you mean by all this, Leo? I'm confused."

"You are not confused by any means. You know exactly what you are doing. Just stop pussyfooting around and do it. It may be your only way out."

Evie looked to Howard. She noticed he did not have his white collar on. How had she not noticed that earlier? Did he wear his collar when he was here before? Why this mattered seemed silly to Evie at this point. Howard had turned toward her, his pressed black shirt, his black trousers, his legs comfortably crossed as he watched her talk to Leo. As Evie walked toward him, she smiled as Howard winked at her in a genuine effort to put her at ease. Evie set the drink down, and bent towards Howard seductively.

"Thank you," Howard said and winked again.

"Anytime, I am always happy to see you."

"How about after work? Will you see me after work?"

"Okay, no, wait, yes, I think it's okay, right?"

"It's okay, really, I'll just drive you home."

"Yes, okay then, if you think it's okay, then okay. You can drive me home. My parents have the kids tonight."

Howard looked at Evie as if no one else was in the room. The key to 17 Prestige Place pressed against his breastbone, he imagined its imprint there for years to come, a kind of branding. Evie was the woman he loved. He loved her more than he loved God. And it was here in Dell's dining room, of all places on earth, that he would deny his love for Jesus, just as Peter had done.

Evie wiped down her station while Howard waited in the car for her. He had gone ahead so as not to draw attention by them leaving together. As Evie crossed Dell's parking lot toward the Cadillac, gusts of wind brought in a light rain. Little tornadoes of leaves, candy wrappers, and dirt swirled up from the asphalt and dissipated as the raindrops grew heavier, denser. Howard was parked under the streetlamp so Evie couldn't avoid seeing him. Howard was having second thoughts. He rolled down the window to speak to Evie before she got in the car.

"I am not sure this is okay. Dear Lord, I'm so very sorry Evie. God has forgiven me, can you?"

Forgiven. His utterance of the word pierced through the rain, encircling her whole being as the rain washed her mascara down her face and soaked her uniform.

"No, Father, it is me who needs forgiveness. I shouldn't have…"

"You did nothing wrong Evie, it's me, I have had these thoughts—thoughts I can't stop, can't pray away. I think about you all the time. I really wanted to help make things better for you and the children. It is wrong of me to be here."

"Father Russo, I'm so sorry, it's just that…," Evie said as she held her purse over her head, the chilly haze of rain gave her shivers.

Howard interrupted now dreading that she will refuse him, "Evie, this is stupid of me. I'm just confused. So sorry. Please get in the car, out of the rain." Evie did not resist this time. She ran around the front of the car. Howard watched her legs glow in the headlights, her head bent forward, her neck long and graceful. He loved her and there was no righting the wrongness of it because it didn't feel wrong, it felt as he always imagined love would feel; mysterious and good. Soaked in the glare of the parking lot light, he looked straight ahead through the windshield, the wipers vigorously working to clear the pelting rain. There was no more self-deprecation, no more questioning of his intentions. Howard swallowed, a blackness had descended into the car, and the weak light was such that he couldn't see his hand in front of his face. As the car door opened, the dome light came on, Evie's face alit, her jaw clenched tight to stop her teeth from chattering.

"You're freezing cold," Howard said as he took off his overcoat and wrapped it around Evie. Evie didn't say anything, instead she pulled the coat tighter around herself, the smell of the wool and his scent warmed her instantly.

"Thank you Father."

"It's Howard, call me Howard now."

"Howard,"Evie said quietly, "Howard it is."

"Yes, like that, I am Howard and you are Evie, and we will make a new life for you and your children."

Howard was surprised to see Evie shake her head yes. He had expected hesitation and a long serious talk to convince her his plan would work. But there was none of that. She simply shook her head yes and they drove away.

Howard reached over and held Evie's hand as they rode along the dark roads and swaying trees. The rain fell, pitiless, without a break all the way down Route 20 until Howard pulled into the drive of 17 Prestige Place. All was still then. Cradled in the branches of the trees that surrounded the house, their secret life began.

Howard held his hand up in a wait sign. Evie waited. He came around to Evie's side of the car and opened the door, as if she were a lady. Howard took the key from his pocket and put it in Evie's hand. She stared at the key in her hand for a long time, a time long enough for Howard to anguish over his plan again, to succumb to his doubt. Could he really make a better life for Evie and her children? Would this sodden path to desire ever be forgiven by God? The intensity in which Howard felt the need to bring parity to his situation, that his love for Evie and her children should equal his love for God as a prerequisite for him to choose one or the other seemed ridiculous at this moment, standing under the clearing sky. Evie reached for Howard's hand, looked into his eyes, then led him to the house, unlocked the door, and stepped inside. Howard followed her, but not before looking to the sky, his final act of contrition, before he shut and locked the door.

To be continued...

AUTHORS NOTE

The sexual abuse of a child by one who has accepted the responsibility to be a representative of God is, as Robert A. McMackin, et al. says in Understanding the Trauma of Clergy Sexual Abuse, "a sinister assault on that person's psychosocial and spiritual well-being. The impact of such a violent betrayal is amplified when the perpetrator is sheltered and supported by a larger religious community."

As many of us remember, the first inklings of the child sex abuse scandal began trickling into the media in the mid-nineties. And it wasn't until 2002 that the full story of the Roman Catholic Church's hidden epidemic of sexual exploitation and child sexual abuse was revealed. We were horrified to learn that between 1950 and 2002, more than 10,000 parishioners, had come forward, with stories of physical, sexual, and emotional abuse at the hands of priests, bishops, and cardinals. And so many of us felt deep sorrow and despair when we learned that others had shared our same fate.

In 2004, The John Jay College Research Team studied the issue. With the findings from the John Jay report, the Catholic Church began to acknowledge the impact of their policies that have resulted in abuse and assaults on individuals, families, and communities, and where their priests have conducted themselves in ways that have produced trauma and sorrow; instead of joy and peace. Clearly there is so much more to do. Nearly twenty years later there are still reports of widespread child sexual abuse by priests. The disturbing stories that have been published in the past five years have shown patterns of deep collusion and webs of illegal activities between local officials, priests, church officials, and even local law enforcement. bishopaccoutability.org keeps tracks of these stories and tries to keeps a full "account" of the bishops' responsibility for the sexual abuse crisis, both individually and collectively. The organization also wants the bishops who have caused the abuse of children and vulnerable adults to be "held accountable."

ACKNOWLEDGEMENTS

My heartfelt and deepest appreciation to everyone who helped bring this novel to publication.

I would like to acknowledge the brave work of *The Journal of Child Sexual Abuse* that dedicated a whole volume to understanding how childhood sexual abuse by Catholic priests impacted individuals immediately, and in the years that followed. And much gratitude to *The Boston Globe* Spotlight reporters who worked tirelessly to uncover the scandal and reported their findings with care and respect for the victims. I would like to acknowledge the dedication of Laurie Goodstein, national religion correspondent for *The New York Times*, who has reported on child sexual abuse by clergy for nearly twenty years. Hopefully these efforts will help families heal by learning to love, trust, and find a new kind of peace in their lives.

I am thankful for the help I received from the knowledgable and thoughtful librarians at the The New York State Library. They helped me identify resources and books to learn the early history of Albany, New York, and of the Catholic Church in the State of New York. I am grateful to have had the opportunity to participate in the The New York State Writer's Institute Community Workshop Program. It provided me with the opportunity to learn from, share with, and connect to excellent writers in my community. I also would like to thank The Troy Arts Center, their wonderful writing program gave me the opportunity to study with an immensely talented and supportive teacher, Lucia Nevai, which led me to my first writing group that included Michael Welch, Sharon Roy, and Judy Cid.

I want to thank Father Dennis Nagi, St Sophia's Orthodox Church for providing the invaluable gift of time and knowledge about Albania, my grandparents, and my heritage, which led me to my grandparent's gravestone where I found it unfinished; missing the date my grandmother passed. My sister researched our grandmother's death and we were able to add the date of her passing and a lovely wreath of flowers in the spring. Come fall, when I went to the graveyard to retrieve the flowers before the first snow, I found tucked in the flowers a business card; our cousin Fotiu Foti had left it. We connected with him and learned of his important and lovely book *Constantinople: The Beautiful City and the Destruction of Its Greek, Armenian, and Jewish Ethnic Communities* which provided the details of place and time to make my grandparents history tangible and accurate. I am forever grateful that he left his card and that we are now in each other's lives.

My Dust Bowl Faeries bandmates, Ryder Cooley, Karen Cole, and Jen DuBois all strong, feminine, creative spirits, and accomplished artists open their hearts to me every week and give me the support, inspiration, and most importantly courage, to freely express myself. I have grown as a person, a writer and a musician because of their friendship and love.

A heartfelt thanks to so many of my dear friends who were supportive and offered encouragement along the way, with special thanks to Violet Moss, Lisa Burke, Laura Duggan, Alice Oldfather, and especially, Christa Parravani, Candace White and Stephanie Boschart, Pat Conover, and Laura Schoenholt who read other versions of this story. Their empathy, understanding, support, and care were just what I needed when I broke my long silence.

I want to especially thank Rudy and Shirley Nelson. They offered patience and encouragement to tell this story, as accomplished and generous writers, I benefited immensely from the great gift of their invitations to story conferences, their confidence in me telling this story, and their love.

Many thanks to Aidan Thompson who edited early drafts and her perspective and keen eye made it possible to move forward in a story with so many time periods. Thank you to Mika Dmytrowska for her creative, thoughtful, and beautiful book design. Thank you to Jen DuBois, who helped copy edit the final draft.

I am lucky to have a dear, wise, and talented sister, Sandra. She encouraged me to tell this story in the best way I could, and to offer my best writing to this work. Her encouragement throughout the process made me feel that finishing this book was possible and important.

I am especially grateful for the loving support from my son, Noah Fowler, who always asks about my writing, reads first drafts, and especially for all the wonderful and countless hours we have spent together learning about, and discussing, the craft of storytelling.

Deep gratitude to all my beloved forever family members, Peter Fowler, Patricia Fennelly, and Kathleen Fennelly, Matthew Fennelly, George and Rose Fowler, Zoe Nelson MacGregor, Rylan Nelson, Tom MacGregor, Kris Nelson, Scott Nelson, Martha Healey Nelson, and Daisy — the kindest, most supportive family ever. I am because we are.

Above all, this book owes its existence to my husband Todd Nelson, who read this novel countless times, and offered his learnings of storytelling from his life-long love for reading. He dedicated many hours to editing the various versions of this story over time — a gift that I will always treasure. I am grateful for his deep understanding of the story I was trying to tell, why I needed to tell it, and my commitment to it being told with compassion, love, and grace. His patience and his encouragement for me to take the time and space I needed to complete this work were always given freely and with love.

And finally this book was possible to write because of the tremendous resources and support I was afforded from groups like Survival Network of Those Abused By Priests (SNAP), Child Rights International Network (CRIN), The Journal of Child Sexual Abuse, and for the brave and courageous reporting of the Boston Spotlight Team who shed light on the darkness that so many of us had lived in. I offer deep gratitude and thanks to my therapists and counselors, mentors and beloveds along the way who loved and cared for me, and helped strengthen my voice, my heart, and my spirit.

RESOURCES FOR CHILD SEXUAL ABUSE SURVIVORS

Survival Network of Those Abused By Priests

http://www.snapnetwork.org

SNAP is 99.9% comprised of volunteers – survivors and supporters – who run and attend support group meetings, answer the Helpline, meet one on one with survivors, pick up phone calls in the middle of the night, and answer dozens of emails a week from victims who need help.

Child Rights International Network

https://www.crin.org/en/home/campaigns/sexual-violence

RAINN (Rape, Abuse & Incest National Network)

https://www.rainn.org and https://www.rainn.org/es

RAINN is the nation's largest anti-sexual violence organization. RAINN created and operates the National Sexual Assault Hotline (800.656.HOPE) in partnership with more than 1,000 local sexual assault service providers across the country and operates the DoD Safe Helpline for the Department of Defense. RAINN also carries out programs to prevent sexual violence, help victims, and ensure that perpetrators are brought to justice.

National Sexual Violence Resource Center

http://www.nsvrc.org

NSVRC provides leadership in preventing and responding to sexual violence through collaboration, sharing and creating resources, and promoting research.

Darkness to Light

http://www.d2l.org

Darkness to Light is guided by the vision of a world free from child sexual abuse, where children can grow up happy, healthy and safe.

Stop the Silence

https://stopthesilence.org/our-work/

The mission of Stop the Silence: Stop Child Sexual Abuse is to expose and stop child sexual abuse and help survivors heal worldwide.

RESOURCES FOR DIRECT ACTION TO HELP STOP OR PREVENT CHILD ABUSE

If you see child sexual abuse or your child has been sexually abused, call 911 or your local police immediately.

If you suspect abuse, call the National Child Abuse Hotline at 1-800-4-A-Child or visit the Child Help Hotline. Trained crisis operators staff the lines 24/7 to answer your questions. If necessary, they will show you how to report in your local area.

Child Abuse Statute of Limitations for each State in the United States
http://angelroar.com/foradults/c-child-abuse-resources-adults/
childabusestatuteoflimitationsbystate

In New York, if you were sexually abused as a minor, you must file your lawsuit within five years of reaching the age of 18. If you wait until after age 23 you will not be permitted to sue your abuser and seek compensation. The statute of limitations for filing a sex abuse or negligence claim against a third party such as a school or a church is three years However, if the acts of negligence occurred when you were a minor, the time period expires three years after your 18th birthday, at age 21.

In matters of child sex abuse, New York has one of the shortest statutes of limitations in the U.S. Some states have eliminated statutes of limitation in criminal and civil child sex abuse actions. A bill to do away with child sex abuse statutes of limitation in both civil and criminal actions in New York has passed in the Assembly but failed in the Senate four times. The bill would also provide for a one-year, one-time window, beginning 60 days after the governor signs the bill, in which people can bring civil lawsuits against individual abusers or institutions in older cases of abuse. Under current New York law, a child sex abuser can evade prosecution or a lawsuit merely because the statute of limitations has expired.

There are many organizations working to overturn this law that you can connect with to learn how to work in your state to eliminate the statute of limitations in both civil and criminal actions for cases of child sexual abuse.

ABOUT THE AUTHOR

JoAnn Stevelos was born and lives in Albany, New York. Her writing explores themes of compassion, estrangement, vulnerability, complex family relationships, lost love, loneliness, and sexual and emotional abuse.

Her next publishing project will be the second novel in this trilogy, called *The Book of Jo*. The third book will be called, *I Am Because We Are*. Each will continue the story of the families in *Howard Be Thy Name*. We discover if the families can heal or remain broken; will they grow together again, or recoil from each other? Will they find a new way of living peacefully, with love, or remain in the past, unable to move on?

JoAnn is the author of *Dream Alibis*, an anthology about finding hope in the aftermath of estrangement, lost love, loneliness, and emotional abuse. The poems segue into *Little Red Wagon*, a play about a family that has created and maintained a divide from a political activist's death by suicide to the present and explores the layers of grief that tethers the family members to one another in conspiratorial silence.

Her story, *Second, You Are Really Nigerian*, was published in Arts and Understanding Literary Magazine and received an Honorable Mention Award from Glimmer Train and the Hudson Valley Writer's Guild. Her essay, *A Voice of My Own*, was published in The Writer. Her work has been quoted in The Guardian, Albany Times Union, Scholastic Magazine, and referenced on the Daily Show, CNN, and in several academic books about childhood obesity, sexual abuse, and bullying. Her blog, *Children at the Table*, is published by Psychology Today.

ABOUT THE FONTS

This book is set in the Candida typeface.

German designer Erbar drew the Candida typeface for the Ludwig & Mayer foundry shortly before his death in 1935. The typeface was released posthumously in 1936. An italic designed by Walter Höhnisch was published the following year and a reworked version was produced in 1945. Bold weights followed in 1951. Thanks to its clarity and readability in small sizes, the Candida family has remained popular in the digital age.

The cover font is Didot.

The typeface family known as Didot was designed by Firmin Didot in Paris in 1783. The Didot types defined the characteristics of the modern (or Didone) roman type style, with their substantial stems flowing into extremely thin hairlines; the serifs are straight across with virtually no bracketing. Because of the very fine hairlines that are characteristic of modern romans, their use was somewhat restricted in metal types.

Designed by Adrian Frutiger for digital technology in 1992, Linotype Didot retains all of the features that make Didot types superior for book work and other text use; like Bodoni, its delicate lines are enhanced in display uses.